3

THE GIRLS OF CANBY HALL®

YOU'RE NO FRIEND OF MINE

EMILY CHASE

SCHOLASTIC INC.
New York Toronto London Auckland Sydney Tokyo

ISBN 0-590-40080-0

12 11 10 9 8 7 6 5 4 3 2   6 7 8 9/8 0/9

Printed in the U.S.A.   01

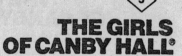

3

THE GIRLS
OF CANBY HALL®

YOU'RE NO
FRIEND OF MINE

THE GIRLS
OF CANBY HALL®

Roommates
Our Roommate is Missing
You're No Friend of Mine
Keeping Secrets
Summer Blues
Best Friends Forever
Four is a Crowd
The Big Crush
Boy Trouble
Make Me a Star
With Friends Like That...
Who's The New Girl?
Here Come the Boys
What's a Girl to Do?
To Tell the Truth
Three of a Kind

CHAPTER ONE

"Oh, blessed no-classes-Sunday," sighed Shelley Hyde, looking up from her books and turning in the chair at her desk to face her two roommates.

On that brisk March morning, with the sun flying in through the window sharp and clear, Faith Thompson was sitting cross-legged on her bed, pensively munching a doughnut topped with strawberry jam, and Dana Morrison, on the floor, was painting her toenails with a pale green polish she had found the last time they had gone into Boston.

"If it wasn't for French," Shelley went on, "I'd be wonderfully happy." She turned back to her textbook and notes. "I'm never going to remember the past subjunctive." She sighed again, ran her hand through her thick, short blond hair, and returned to doing the homework that had to be ready for first period the next day. "At school back home I never had to study past subjunctives."

1

"That's why you left Iowa, Shelley," said Dana, smiling down at her toes.

"It's part of horizons," Faith added.

In their first weeks at Canby Hall, Shelley had told Faith and Dana that her parents had wanted her to leave Pine Bluff and come to school in Massachusetts to "broaden her horizons." She had confided to the girls, however, that her parents really had meant leave Paul, her boyfriend, but Dana and Faith always seemed to forget that part.

"For the millionth time, I'd like to say I'm sorry I ever told you two anything," Shelley said.

"Just kidding." Faith smiled over at her.

Dana was absorbed in her toenails. "I don't think green looks so good after all," she pronounced after eyeing her feet carefully.

Shelley once more turned away from her French book. "Thank goodness you decided that. I didn't want to say anything, because you're so . . . well, you know, you're the *chic* New Yorker and supposed to know about fashion, but honestly, *green* nail polish!"

"Okay," Dana said. "I've tried it. Now it goes!" She studied her toes a moment longer.

"I wish I were eating a soft bagel," Faith said wistfully and took another bite of her doughnut. "I may just have to go out and get some."

She unwrapped herself from her cross-legged position on the bed and walked over to the window. "Looks like the perfect bagel day."

"If you're really going, get some peanut butter, too. We're very low," Shelley said. She left the desk and went to examine their private Sunday breakfast set out on a footlocker in the middle of the floor: cookies, doughnuts, a slice of cold pizza left over from the night before, candy, cheese, strawberry jam, crackers, and the almost empty jar of peanut butter that Shelley picked up, tilted, and showed to Faith. Drinks were on the windowsill: a six-can-high, ten-can-wide pyramid of diet soda.

Faith looked across the park in front of their dorm, over toward the woods where the trees, rustling against the spring breezes, were already promising green buds, green leaves — and the end of the school year. *One full school year at Canby Hall,* Faith thought, remembering how, when she had arrived, the trees had been on fire with orange, red, and yellow leaves — the full autumn colors of New England — so different from Washington, D.C., her home.

It had been so awful coming into the empty, bare, bleak room. The prospect of sharing it with two complete strangers — who would probably be white — had made her feel upset before she even got started.

Faith glanced over her shoulder for a moment at Dana and Shelley, who were so familiar now, and then she went back to her thoughts.

When she had first met them she had felt like curling up and crying, except that crying had become something she didn't do anymore. She had cried all her tears after her wonderful father, Police Officer Walter Thompson, had been shot to death halting a bank robbery. She would always, forever, miss him. She knew her mother missed him even more but her mother was still able to give warmth and love at the agency where she was a social worker. Faith had spoken to her mother the night before and heard the family news; Sarah, her sister, a freshman at Georgetown University, was getting all A's and B's and that her brother Richie, who was almost thirteen, was planning a big birthday party that month.

A pale gray car was slowly turning in through the sturdy wrought-iron gates of the school, and Faith watched it drive along the maple grove. Then she turned back to the room, picked up her down jacket, and checked her wallet.

"Bagels. Peanut butter. Anything else?" Faith asked.

"Polish remover, if you can get it, please. I've lost mine," Dana said.

John Morrison, smoothing his hair with his hand, continued to drive slowly toward the school buildings. He admired the woods on his right, the orchard, and the meadow that lay behind it, but he was balancing it in his mind against other scenery: tropical, lush, maybe more beautiful than this perfect New England setting. He was glad his daughter Dana was at Canby Hall, but he was worried: What would Dana's reaction be to what he'd come to tell her?

As he drove toward Baker House, the oldest of the three Canby Hall dormitories, he saw a tall, thin, attractive, black girl. She was striding down the roadway, clutching a pale blue down jacket against the sharp breeze. He thought she was one of Dana's roommates, the girl from Washington. Faith Thompson?

"Faith?" he called out.

The girl stopped and looked back at him. "Oh . . . Mr. Morrison?"

"That's right. Dana around?"

Faith came over to the car. "Hi. Sure. She's in the dorm."

"Good," he said briskly.

A faintly puzzled expression flew over Faith's face, but she didn't say anything.

"She didn't know I was coming," said Mr. Morrison, answering the expression. "I'm a surprise."

"She'll like that," said Faith, smiling.

With a wave, Mr. Morrison drove past the dorm to the visitors' parking area, under a row of wind-tossed trees. Faith watched the car drive out of sight, wondering why Dana's father had appeared so suddenly.

* * *

Gloria Palmer, the week's dorm monitor, tapped on the door of Room 407 and walked in. "Visitor for you, Dana."

"Can't be. I'm not expecting anybody," Dana said.

"How about your father?" Gloria asked.

"I'm *definitely* not expecting my father." Dana paused. "Is he here?" she asked with surprise.

"Well, there's a really terrific-looking man downstairs in the lounge and he *says* he's your father," Gloria answered.

"Must be, then. Wow!" Dana got up, pulled her sweater over her jeans, and made a quick jab at her hair with her fingers.

"Dana, your toes!" protested Shelley.

Dana laughed, and barefooted, green-toe-nailed, ran downstairs.

Her father was standing, gazing out of the great window of the large downstairs lounge, holding a cup of coffee. Scattered around the room were the usual Sunday sprawl of girls and their thick Boston and New York Sunday newspapers. A buffet table held pitchers of fruit juice, plates of doughnuts, and milk sent over from the dining hall; the full coffee urn was courtesy of Alison Cavanaugh, the housemother.

Dana studied her father's back, straight as it always was, in a worn, wonderful tweed jacket. Dana remembered when it was new and he'd brought it back from England when her parents had gone on a vacation there, before they had had those awful fights, before the divorce. She wondered if her father was wearing that particular jacket for some significant reason. She tried to squash her persistent hope that her parents would get together again.

"Dad!" she called out.

He turned, his bright eyes happy to see her. He quickly put down the cup and held his arms out. Dana ran into them, feeling the safe, contented warmth she always experienced with her father.

"Hi, honey. How's everything?" John Morrison, much as he tried not to, sounded nervous. Dana picked up her father's tone immediately. She looked suspicious.

"I love to see you, Dad, and I love unexpected visitors, but what's up?"

"Can't a father come and visit his favorite older daughter when there's a spare Sunday?" Mr. Morrison asked, not looking at Dana.

"No!" Dana said. "*You* don't do things like that."

"Smart girl," he said, looking sheepish. "You're right. I'm here on a mission, but it can wait." He studied her. "I like the toes," he said, changing the subject. "Look, it's sort of lunch time, isn't it? Have you had lunch?"

"Well, I've been eating breakfast all morning," Dana said, patting her stomach.

"How about dessert then. Do you have a special place you like?" John Morrison asked.

"The Tutti-Frutti is great," Dana said, after thinking a minute. "I'll go sign out. I'll just be a minute."

Dana ran to the staircase, then turned around, a small worried frown between her eyebrows. "Everything's all right, isn't it, Dad?"

"Everything's fantastic, honey." He smiled reassuringly.

Dana bit her lip for a second. "Be right back," she said.

Upstairs, she poked her head through the door, checking in with Shelley.

"I'm off with my Dad," she said. "Sorry to run out on you, but Faith'll be back soon."

Shelley was halfheartedly trying to concentrate on her French homework.

Dana hurriedly scrawled her name on the sign-out sheet taped on the outside of their door. Along with the room number, there were artistic renditions of their names. Each roommate had done her own.

Dana had written her name in an elaborate, arty print; Faith's was in fat, balloony letters; Shelley had cut letters out of magazines and pasted them together — "like a ransom note," Dana had said. Shelley had actually been kidnapped only a month earlier and didn't think Dana's comment was very funny. It had been an awful experience, and

Shelley still woke up at night shivering in a cold sweat.

The sign-out sheet on the door required each girl to write where she was going and when she expected to be back, and there was a space to fill in when she actually got back.

"If a girl isn't back within an hour or so of when she's expected, I begin to worry, so be on time!" Alison Cavanaugh said to all her dorm girls.

CHAPTER TWO

At the Tutti-Frutti, Dana ordered her favorite concoction: a marshmallow, lemon, and walnut sundae. She sat facing her father, watching him closely. Each time Dana saw her Dad, she missed his being with her mother; she loved them both and it killed her that they didn't love *each other* anymore. The divorce had been almost three years ago, and she still couldn't get used to it.

"How's Eve?" she asked politely.

Eve was the latest woman friend of her father's. Dana had met her the last time she was in New York.

"I'm going to marry her, Dana," he said.

Dana gave her father her full, solemn attention, but she remained absolutely silent.

He smiled gently. "You're not too surprised, are you?"

Dana shook her head. "No," she said.

Her voice was peculiarly low and hoarse, and she had a terrible sinking feeling, but her father's face was glowing. He looked so happy — she remembered how awful it had been the last time her parents were together with her, at her farewell breakfast at the coffee shop in Grand Central Station before they saw her off on the train to Canby Hall. It had been total *disaster*.

"She's a very nice woman, Dana," her father said.

"I guess . . . you wouldn't want to . . . you'd only choose a nice woman." Dana clenched her hands in her lap.

Her father reached across the table and put his hand against her cheek. "All the women in my family are nice women. You . . . your sister . . ."

"Including Mom?" Dana asked eagerly.

"Of course," her father answered, too quickly.

The waiter came with their orders, and Dana caught another expression on her father's handsome face. She leaned forward.

"There's more to it," he said nervously. "Listen to this one, honey. . . ."

"Listening," Dana said, looking down at her ice cream.

"I'm being transferred out of New York for a year."

Dana felt a shock wave. Getting married *and* going away?

"The agency's involved in a new merger, and they need a top man, which is me, to set up the combined operation." John Morrison smiled proudly.

Dana knew her father was a vice-president of Mason, Guerrero, O'Regan, and Wright, a big advertising agency, but sometimes, like now, she didn't have a clue, not really, of what that actually meant, what he did at work.

"Are you ready for where they're sending me for a year?" he asked.

"I guess so," Dana said wanly.

"Honolulu, Hawaii."

"Hawaii!" Dana repeated, stunned.

Her father leaned back with a grin as broad as his whole face. "Isn't that something? Work all day, dance the hula all evening."

"Hawaii," Dana said again with disbelief. "Dad . . ."

"Yeah, honey?"

"Dad, that's 6,000 miles away." Her voice shook slightly.

"A long way, Dana. A very long way from Canby Hall, and that's a big part of part two of this announcement. Eve and I both very much want you to come and live with us for that year, Dana." He paused. "I promise you'll like Eve, Dana. The longer you know her, I promise the more you'll like her."

Dana's spoon clattered against the dish. "Come *with* you! To Hawaii? Oh, Dad."

"That's quite a decision to make isn't it?" he said gently.

It *was* — even for cool Dana.

"Eve's going to write to you, Dana, but I wanted to talk to you first." Her father watched her intently.

"Can I think about it?" Dana asked.

"Of course." Her father reached over and touched her hand.

"What about Maggie?" Dana's thirteen-year-old sister was in school in New York.

"You first, honey. You're older." He looked away and then back at her. "I know it's awfully fast. Very sudden."

Dana nodded.

"It has been for me, too. Marrying Eve's been on my mind for a long time, but I wanted to wait. I thought during the summer you and Maggie would get to know her better, and both of you could grow into the idea. But this Hawaii thing changed all that. I have to be there off and on already. I'm going at the end of this week, for instance, for ten days or so. I *have* managed to delay the permanent move until June, but I'll have to be there more than here from now on. It's tough on Eve."

"Mmm," Dana said, hardly concerned with Eve.

"Anyway, I'll be back in June. A June wedding . . ."

He sounded like a delighted young boy, Dana noticed with astonishment. "Then all of us will go back to Honolulu. If you want to — I hope you *will* want to, and so does

Eve. There's a good school in Honololu, really good, I made careful inquiries, and Hawaii itself . . . wait till you . . . . You'll love it, honey . . . . climate . . . beautiful. . . . We want you . . . . You'll love it. . .love it . . ."

Her father's voice faded out. Dana couldn't hear it anymore. She was remembering Eve when they met. Dana had come to pick up her father at his office, and Eve had come *dancing* in — this woman with floppy, flowing, orange-yellow hair, a khaki split-skirt, and ankle-high boots. She was young, so much younger than her mother that Dana almost didn't believe her dad — but his voice, the way he looked, had clued her in. He had said, "This is Eve. I want you to know each other." They went out of the office together, the three of them — Eve the art director, her father, and Dana.

Married.

Hawaii.

Later, Dana closed the dorm door behind her and leaned against it, feeling so disoriented she needed the door for support. Baker Hall was quiet; her father had dropped her off at seven-thirty, just as Study Hours began, and she knew she ought to hurry up to her room. Sophomores had to be in their rooms, the library, or the language lab, through Study Hours, seven-thirty to nine-thirty. Only when you were a junior or senior could you go to other rooms and study with friends or curl up alone, all alone, in the now-empty lounge, as Dana so longed to do. It was as though she could hear the thumping of her heartbeat. Dad-married-not-to-Mom. Dad married-not-to-Mom. Eve-thump-Eve-thump-Eve-thump-Eve-thump.

She wasn't quite ready to share this news with Faith and Shelley; she had to digest it herself first.

At the end of the weekend, on Sunday evening before Study Hours, each girl in the dorm who had been away had to sign in on a sheet on the bulletin board outside of Alison Cavanaugh's apartment. The girls had to sign in, tap on Alison's door, say hello to Alison, and receive — without knowing it — Alison's decisive "quick look."

After two years as the houseparent at Baker House, Alison's quick look was a flicker, a dart of her eyes while she was calmly sipping or offering tea, hot chocolate, or a glass of milk. Or it was when she was glancing up, seemingly casual, from a book. It told Alison instantly whether a girl had had a happy weekend or not. She could tell if a girl returning to school from a weekend at home was coming back reluctantly, was feeling homesick, or was relieved. She knew if a girl was troubled — hadn't eaten, hadn't slept.

Alison's fleeting look at the beginning of the term had gotten Dana, Faith, and Shelley into her apartment quickly to sit down and settle what promised to be a first-class hate among the three new roommates. With Alison's help, the hurtful misunderstandings had eased away, and the girls had become close. Since then, any quick look at the girls in Room 407 hadn't shown any serious problems.

Most of the Baker House girls tapped at Alison's door on Sunday evenings, whether they'd been away or not. And Dana did, too. Alison looked at Dana and knew something had happened. The usually totally with-it girl seemed a million miles away . . . and her eyes — was Dana crying?

"Cup of tea, Dana?" Alison asked, pouring a cup from the ever-ready electric pot and handing it to Dana. Then, gently, "Sit down."

Even in her unexpectedly disturbed state, Dana found herself smiling briefly, admiring Alison. It was a brave attempt, but a weak smile.

"I guess you can tell I'm in shock," she said. "You see, my dad . . ." and she poured it all out.

". . . so I think I better go home. I mean, I want to sign out for home next weekend. I want to see my mom."

Faith and Shelley would have been surprised to hear smooth, cool Dana sound so like a little girl. Shelley might have reacted like that, Faith would have tried to cover up her feelings, but Dana always was in control.

"I think that's a good idea," Alison said quickly.

"Mmm," Dana agreed, biting into one of

Alison's special good-nutrition cookies. Alison was unpredictable, sometimes serving Tab and rich brownies and sometimes insisting on health snacks.

Alison curled up in her comfortable chair, her large horn-rimmed glasses slipping down her nose as usual, her manner calm and reassuring.

"Well, you really do have an important decision to make. The best thing to do is just take your time about it. Talk it up. Think it all the way through."

"I will. I promise." There was a long pause. "It isn't that Eve isn't nice, you know," Dana said. "She really is."

Now it was Alison's turn to munch a cookie and say, "Mmm."

"But's she's so young. . . . I mean, she has to be . . . my mother's practically forty, you know. I don't think Eve's even thirty yet. . . ." Dana looked away, her eyes filling up.

Then she gave in to the force of her feelings, beat her fist against the arm of the sofa. "It's not fair! It's just not fair. He should marry my mother again. That's who he should marry." And the tears flowed.

After a while, she sniffled her last sniffle, patted her green eyes, and pulled her shiny, long dark hair like a curtain over the side of her face to try to disguise the tearfulness.

"I mean, the point is, even if my dad doesn't want to marry my mom again — and I know Mom can't stand to be with him for more than ten minutes, so she probably doesn't want to marry him, anyway . . ."

Dana hesitated for a moment. "I mean, granted all that, I don't really know Eve. How could I go so far away to live with someone I don't really know? What if we can't stand each other? What if she's one of those people who hates the way I throw my clothes around the room? It drives Shelley bonkers."

"Good questions," Alison said softly.

"Although I'm sure they wouldn't be inviting me if they didn't expect we would all get along."

"At first it didn't seem too easy to get along with Faith and Shelley, did it?" Again Alison spoke softly.

"That's right," Dana said. She paused and another thought struck her. "It would mean leaving Faith and Shelley for our whole junior year. We're a good set of roommates. We're good *friends*."

"Yes, you are," said Alison.

"And there's Bret," Dana went on. "I still think he's very special, Alison. I mean, we're definitely still going together. Bret Harper's reformed, you know. He's a one-woman guy now, and I'm it."

"I did have some idea of that, Dana," Alison said with a smile. She had warned Dana about nearby Oakley Prep's best-known heartbreaker soon after Bret started rushing Dana. Later she conceded that Bret's pattern had changed.

"Well, if I went to Hawaii, I certainly would miss Bret," Dana said softly. She took a deep breath, sighed, and then tried to laugh a little. "On the other hand," she went on, "there's the dining hall. Would I mind swapping our dining-hall food for breadfruit, snow for hibiscus, and jogging for the hula?" Dana smiled.

Alison glanced at the clock on the mantle. "Better get to your room now, Dana. Study Hours are half over already. Remember, take your time about all this. Catch your breath."

"Where *were* you?!" Shelley exclaimed, pouncing on Dana.

"Oh, talking with Alison," Dana answered evasively.

Faith looked at Dana carefully. She had been concerned all evening. Parents just didn't come to school without warning. And now Dana looked strange and distracted. Shelley and Faith waited for Dana to say something more, but Dana was silent.

"Whatever it is," Faith said finally, "it'll be all right, Dana."

"Sure it will," Dana answered.

It was confusing, upsetting, to see confident Dana withdraw in front of their eyes. Dana slipped some tapes into her Walkman, clapped on the headphones, and flopped onto her bed, facing the wall.

CHAPTER
THREE

The next morning, as the girls were getting dressed for breakfast, Dana was ready to talk over her problem with Faith and Shelley. Somehow, with them, the sun shining, and Canby Hall looking its springtime prettiest, the situation didn't seem insurmountable.

"It's an awful decision to have to make," Dana said. "How can I leave you two, and yet . . ."

Faith and Shelley were silent, overwhelmed by what Dana had just told them.

"You mean you might leave us?" Shelley asked breathlessly. "How could I stand it?"

Faith just looked at Dana for a moment. "I can't imagine what it would be like here without you. I can't imagine another roommate, and yet it is such an exciting possibility for you to go to Hawaii."

As they left Baker House to go to the dining room, the girls linked arms, as if holding on to each other would prolong their togetherness. There didn't seem to be words to describe what they were feeling — the fear of separation, their anxiety about a new roommate for Shelley and Faith, and a whole new world for Dana.

Faith could imagine her mother marrying a man who had a daughter, going to live faraway for a year, and inviting the daughter to live with them. It was something her warm, loving mother would do.

"I think it's very . . . well, loving, you know, that they want you to come with them, especially for Eve," Faith said.

"Yeah, but," Dana said.

Shelley, whose mother and father were such a *unit* she almost couldn't conceive of parents who were divorced, walked along quietly listening.

"I'm going to read up on Hawaii after classes today," Dana said.

Shelley stopped short on the path. "Oh, wow! I was so busy doing my French yesterday that I forgot that after classes today are tryouts for the spring play. I only read through the play three times. That's not enough!"

"It's enough," Faith said.

"Lunchtime — I'll work on it at lunch." Shelley looked relieved.

"Okay," said Faith. "Hang in there, Dana," she said sympathetically as they went into the dining hall and joined the crowded cafeteria line. "Whichever decision you make will be okay, you know. Hawaii just can't be too bad, but there's nothing wrong with being here again next year." Her voice broke slightly, and she quickly cleared her throat, trying to hide her feelings.

There were already a dozen girls in the Round Table Room in the basement of the library when Shelley arrived, out of breath from running as fast as she could. Her last class had been in the Science Building, exactly on the other side of Main Building, the farthest building of all from the library. Thespians, the school acting group, always met in the Round Table Room, which had a small raised stage at one end and, as the central piece of furniture, a battered, enormous old round oak table almost splintery with the many initials and dates that Canby Hall Thespians had carved deep into its surface through the years. Ms. Mac — Mrs. Mac-Pherson in real life and in English class where she taught Shakespeare, but Ms. Mac at Thespians — clapped her hands for attention.

"All right, girls. All right. Everybody sit down."

The roomful of girls flopped into the straight-backed chairs circling the round table. Those who couldn't find chairs — like Shelley and Julia Baron, a junior she knew slightly — sank onto the carpeted floor, backs against the wall, legs stretched out.

"We're here to read for the girls' parts in the spring play, right?"

A chorus of "Right's" came from the girls.

"The boys' parts will be played, as usual, by boys from Oakley Prep and, this year, by a boy from Greenleaf High School in town, too," Ms. Mac said.

That was news! Oakley Prep was a neighboring boys' school. The two schools always exchanged actors: Oakley boys played the male parts in Canby Hall plays; Canby Hall girls played in Oakley productions. There was usually a mixer for new students at the two schools at the start of the year, so Canby Hall girls often ended up knowing many more Oakley Prep boys than boys from town. Now a town boy was going to be in their play.

"But we won't worry about boys now," said Ms. Mac.

The girls laughed at that.

"You know the play very well because you all had the weekend to study it. Right?"

"Right!" came from the girls.

"We'll read act II, scene 2 — all the women are in that scene. It's page twenty-four in your copies of the play."

"Ms. Mac runs these things like a martinet," Julia whispered to Shelley in a faintly bored voice.

"Um-hum," Shelley whispered back. She

wasn't sure what martinet meant.

"Page twenty-four. Get it?" said Ms. Mac.

"Got it!" called out the girls. Most of the girls, the older members of Thespians, had been Thespians long enough to know the response.

"Good!" exclaimed Ms. Mac.

"Get it? Got it! Good!" It was Ms. Mac's favorite joke, an old routine, she said, from a Danny Kaye movie. Ms. Mac had been an actress on Broadway once.

Shelley loved the give-and-take of the routine. She was enjoying this small, introductory taste of Thespians. It seemed so much more professional than the Dramatic Society in Pine Bluff ever had been. Suddenly she felt really eager, more than she had before, really determined to be in the play.

"What part do you want?" she whispered to Julia.

"Oh, Laura, probably."

Shelley smiled tentatively. "Me, too," she said. "Laura."

"Oh, well," said Julia, still with her bored tone, shrugging her shoulders a little. "It'll probably go to a senior."

"All right, for the first reading . . ." Ms. Mac's voice cut through the whispers. She looked at the list in her hand, studied the faces of the girls around the table and on the carpeted floor, and made her choices.

"Ann, read Laura, please. And you —

Amanda Keefe, isn't it — please read . . . yes,
and let's see . . ."

Again, her eyes went around the room,
pausing at Shelley — which made Shelley
catch her breath — moving on, coming back
to Shelley, and then away again.

"And Julia, will you read Emily, please?
All right, girls, top of page." A rustle of pages
turning, girls finding comfortable positions.

" 'Is that really what you wanted to tell me,
Laura?' " Ms. Mac read in a flat voice.
"Amanda? Go!"

" 'Is that really what you wanted to tell me,
Laura?' " read Amanda Keefe. Shelley leaned
forward, following the reading with great
intensity.

When the readings were over, Shelley left
the Round Table Room in a daze. Something
about the afternoon she had just spent —
the gathering of girls, the good spirit that
seemed to flow through them and to and from
Ms. Mac, the curious pleasure she had gotten
when she had read for one of the parts and
had suddenly become not Shelley but someone
different altogether — almost overwhelmed
her. As she made her way toward the dining
hall, crisp little breezes stung her face and
chilled her slightly, just enough to make her
hurry. Once in the dining hall, she made her
way along the cafeteria line with groups of
other girls and pushed her tray forward. She

wasn't hungry — she couldn't eat a thing, she was sure she couldn't — but to be on the safe side, she accepted the pork chop with gravy and took two of the big, crisp rolls. The dazed sensation changed, and she felt a rising excitement she wanted to share with Dana and Faith. Walking toward the tables, carrying her tray, she felt she was a different girl from the Shelley who had parted from her two roommates at the beginning of the day.

By the time she was out of her daze completely and her excitement had reached great heights, Shelley was with Faith and Dana at a table with several other girls. Casey Flint was there, Jackie Adams and Gloria Palmer from Baker House, and several other girls. There were too many people for the intimate conversation Shelley wanted, a conversation in which she could talk about the great experience she had had.

After dinner, the girls walked in a group back to Baker House. Dana and Jackie, who were both in choir, started singing a two-part round that the other girls soon picked up. They trooped across the campus singing together, and there was something in the sound of the music that moved Shelley. It was as though everything in her life was about to change, as though time was suspended for a moment. It made her even more eager to talk to her roommates.

Finally, Shelley, Dana, and Faith were back in Room 407, settling down for Study Hours. The moment had come for Shelley to share her strange, important new feelings with her dearest friends — with Dana, with Faith.

"Something happened to me today," Shelley announced to the two other girls.

"What happened, Shel?" Faith asked, settling herself cross-legged on her bed, her American history book on her lap, her glasses slipping down on her nose as they sometimes did when she was reading.

Shelley expected Dana to respond, too, but Dana had not moved. She was at her desk with her books open in front of her, but she seemed to be gazing inside herself intently.

"Dana," said Shelley plaintively, in a small, hurt voice. "Don't you want to hear, too?"

Dana blinked, came back from her reverie, turned, and waved at Shelley. "Sure. I'm sorry. Thinking about my problem. What is it?"

"Well, something simple, really. It's just, well, I have really found what I want to do with my life."

"Ah," Dana said. Dana was now altogether with her friends. She turned in her chair, green eyes lively, long brown hair falling like silk to her shoulders.

"What do you want to do, Shelley?"

"I thought you'd never ask," Shelley an-

swered and then, through all the seriousness
and the intensity of her feeling, realized how
funny she was being and collapsed into giggles. In the process of doubling over, she
stumbled on one of Faith's new green
sneakers lying in the middle of the room.
Shelley picked it up by a lace and held it
aloft with a great exaggerated sigh. Shelley
despaired of her roommates' tidiness. They
were clean, she acknowledged — took plenty
of showers, washed their hair often enough,
sometimes twice a day — but they were extremely messy. Thanks to them, Room 407
did not always pass muster on the weekly
houseparent tour of inspection.

Shelley had often declared that her aim in
life was to marry her hometown boyfriend
and live a happy housewife's life just like
her mother. She now slipped into her familiar
manner as Miss Future Homemaker.

"You're supposed to have two of these,
Faith, and in the closet," she said.

"But I'm wearing one, Shelley," Faith said.

"Oh, I give *up*."

"So do I," Faith said. "Do we get the big
news, or do we start to study the way we're
supposed to during Study Hours?"

"All right." Shelley paused dramatically.
"Are you ready? My big news is that I *think*
I intend to spend the rest of my life as an
actress."

Faith laughed out loud.

"Do you suppose Shelley got a part in the

spring play?" Dana asked innocently, teasingly.

"Well, I think so," said Faith. "What do you think?"

"I think so," said Dana, and both girls, as though on a signal, jumped up, one from the bed, the other from her desk chair, and together they threw their arms around Shelley.

"A toast!" Dana proposed, taking three cans of Tab from the pyramid on the windowsill. Faith swiftly picked three Styrofoam cups from the tower of cups swaying by her bed. Soon the girls were lifting foaming cups of Tab.

"To Shelley's career in the theater," declared Faith.

"What part'd you get, Shel?"

"Emily."

"Well, good!" Faith said.

"I wanted Laura."

"Sure you did. But Laura's the lead, isn't it?" said Dana.

"Well . . . second lead."

"And it went to a senior, didn't it?" Dana persisted.

"Yes."

"How many other sophomores got parts?"

"I was the only one," Shelley confessed with a sheepish, happy smile. "After all," she continued, "I did play the lead in a play in the Dramatic Society in Pine Bluff." She paused. "And you know what else?" she said slowly. "I think I'm going to change the way

I spell my name. From now on, I'm going to spell it S-h-e-l-l-e. It's much more, well, fitting for the theater that way," she said.

Shelley didn't add that even in Pine Bluff she had longed to adopt that spelling. She had thought it was sophisticated, but she also had suspected that all her friends would think it was hysterically funny. She had never acquired the courage even to try it on them.

"Horizons!" exclaimed Dana. "Good for you if that's what you want to do!"

CHAPTER FOUR

The instant Study Hours were over that evening, Dana quickly went down to the Lower Hall, where the telephones were, to call her mother. As she had told Alison, she wanted to see her mother and discuss face-to-face with her this gigantic problem her father had created. After she had dropped all her coins in the phone box and dialed, she heard the familiar ring of their phone in New York and then an answer — and *then* she was very disappointed. It was her mother's voice, but on the telephone answering machine: "I'm sorry we are not able to answer your call. If you will please leave your name and a message, we will get back to you as soon as possible," said the voice.

Dana almost burst out crying.

"Oh, Mom, why aren't you there? Where's Maggie?" she wailed to the answering machine. "It's me, Dana. I'm coming to New

York next weekend, next Friday. Dad was here. Do you know his news ? He said —"

Dana heard the little click on the other end, which meant she had used up all the message time on the answering machine. She hung up disconsolately and went back to 407.

"Everything okay?" Faith asked.

"Nobody home," Dana answered, the disappointment echoing in her voice. "But I left a message on the machine. I told my mother I was coming. It *will* be okay."

"What machine?" asked Shelley.

"Oh, my mom has a telephone answering machine. It takes a message if she or my sister isn't home," Dana explained.

"Oh," said Shelley.

Faith, listening, had a feeling that telephone answering machines were not very common in Pine Bluff, Iowa.

For Dana, knowing that she would be home at the end of the week made the next few days easier; her mother would help her — or make the decision for her. With that understood, Dana decided she could push away the whole idea that her father had presented to her.

"I'm just not going to think about it," she said to Shelley the next day as they came out of English class together.

"About what?" Shelley asked.

"About *what*?! Shelley, about whether I'm going to go off and live with my father and his new wife in Hawaii . . ." Dana was exasperated. Shelley seemed to be in another world.

"Forgive me, Dana. I was thinking about something else," Shelley said dreamily.

"Let me guess. The construction of a sonnet?" That's what their last hour of English had been devoted to.

"No," Shelley answered seriously. "About the read-through of the spring play this afternoon. The whole cast is reading, boys and all."

"I *should* have guessed," Dana said.

"No reason to," said Shelley. "You should've been thinking about your own situation."

"Oh, Shelley!" exclaimed Dana, ready to shake her friend back to her senses, which Dana was sure Shelley had lost. "I just finished saying I'm *not* going to think about . . . oh, never mind." Dana laughed. "Go off to your rehearsal, Shel, and have a good time."

"See you later, alligator," Shelley said.

Dana stood stock-still as Shelley turned and started walking toward the Library.

"Shelley Hyde," Dana called out. Shelley — and four other girls — stopped and looked back inquiringly.

"Promise never, *never* to say that again."

"I posalutely won't," Shelley said. Dana groaned, and they both laughed as they went their separate ways.

* * *

Shelley had come to Canby Hall from Pine Bluff absolutely certain that she would never look at another boy, never think about another boy. Having sworn true and faithful love to Paul back home, there could never be another boy in her life. But when she walked into the Round Table Room, the first person she saw was the town boy Tom Stevenson, and she forgot that certainty. Tom, taller than anybody else in the room, was talking with other members of the cast, at ease and the center of attention. Shelley's reaction to him startled her. For someone deeply committed to another boy as Shelley was to Paul, she found herself surprisingly unable to look away from Tom, no matter how hard she tried. She particularly couldn't look away from him when, at Ms. Mac's command, he and the other boys and girls began to sit down at the round table. Her staring caught his eye, and with a crooked smile, he gestured to her to come sit in the empty chair next to him. The reading began before she had quite caught her breath, but by the time they began to talk to each other, she decided she felt poised and sophisticated.

It was a short conversation.

"You're prettier than your pictures," Tom whispered.

She knew he meant the pictures of her that had been in the newspaper after her kidnapping.

"I think so, too," Shelley answered with

what she hoped was an amusing shrug. "I rather thought I looked like a scared goose." She laughed. "Guess why."

"Because you were?" he asked, smiling that crooked smile.

Shelley felt all her sophistication collapse. That was exactly the reason.

Shelley still was a little shaky about the kidnapping, even if it had turned her into a minor school celebrity. People she didn't recognize greeted her warmly when they passed her on campus and in the dining hall. Especially on weekends, when parents might be visiting, she could recognize the signs: heads bent, whispered words, eyes turning to look at her. At the tryout, even Ms. Mac had made note of the kidnapping.

"Remembering your feelings at that time may well help you understand and communicate the emotion you need to express in your big third-act scene," Ms. Mac had said. Shelley only felt uncomfortable. She didn't see any connection between a scene in which she was supposed to be angry and the terror she had felt being held captive.

That evening, she told Faith and Dana that the town boy, Tom Stevenson, was enormously interesting "and fairly good-looking, too," she added as casually as she could.

"Like how?" asked Faith, knowing that Shelley was longing to be asked.

"Well, tall. Very tall. Probably actually six feet. I have to crane my head back to look up at him." She made a sound that was almost an indulgent laugh.

"Why, Shelley," Dana said, "I distinctly remember your saying that one of the things you loved about Paul was that he wasn't too tall."

"That's different," said Shelley.

"I see," Dana said, grinning.

"The girls at rehearsal thought he was terrific," Shelley said. She paused, thinking of Paul, not daring to say out loud that *she* had thought Tom was terrific, too. "He noticed me right away. He told me that he remembered seeing pictures of me in the newspaper last month — during the kidnapping." She paused again and then added, again casually, "He, uh, said I was prettier than my pictures."

She didn't tell them that his whisper had seemed to be sheer magic. "He caught my interest," she said instead.

"You told us that," Dana said.

"Well, he did. That's the only way I can describe it."

"I think she thinks he's interesting," Dana said sarcastically to Faith.

"He caught my interest, that's all." Shelley was annoyed with Dana.

"Tell us about it," Dana retorted. "How tall did you say he was? You didn't mention the length of his eyelashes."

Shelley didn't think Dana was funny, neither did Faith, and Dana herself was shocked that she had been so sharp with Shelley. *I'd better get home quickly,* she thought. She felt unusually disturbed.

Dana's peace of mind was not improved when she was called to the telephone at nine-thirty, exactly at the end of Study Hours.

"It was Eve," she said to Faith as she hung up.

Faith was on the long line that had formed to use the phone. After Study Hours, Faith had gone down to telephone home but not fast enough to be first on line. There were three phone booths in a row at Baker House and when Study Hours were over, there always was a mad dash for them.

Faith was waiting to call home because tomorrow was her brother's birthday and she was going to have to be at the school paper late afternoon and into the evening. She didn't know how long it would take to lay out the photographic essay she had prepared for the next issue.

Faith had come to Canby Hall hoping to get on the school paper as a photographer — hoping, at least, for a few trial assignments. To her surprise and pleasure, she had been taken on immediately, the *Clarion*'s only two photographers having graduated the year before. Since her long-range ambition was to be a professional news photographer, the work on the paper very important to her. Still, even the paper couldn't keep Faith from her phone call home. She *had* to wish a happy birthday to her only brother, whom she missed very much. She had knitted Richie a big blue and white scarf. Just thinking about Richie, her sister, and her mother made Faith feel warm inside. Canby Hall was part of her family's master plan — the best possible education, work, and life accomplishment for each of them — but sometimes Faith hated being away.

A phone was free.

"Hold it a second, Dana," Faith said, stepping into the booth and then, "I *knew* it," as she came out again. "I get enough dimes to sink a battleship; I wait two hours — well, twenty minutes — for a free phone, well, what happens? The line's busy. Oh, well, I'll try again later. Or maybe crack of dawn tomorrow. *That* will surprise Richie."

The girls walked toward the Ping-Pong room. Almost nobody in Baker House ever played Ping-Pong; it was a sort of reverse pride thing. There were the table, racquets, and Ping-Pong balls set up and waiting, but nobody used them. The Ping-Pong room was a natural place to drift to, though. It was where all the candy and soft drink machines were. Alison had supervised the contents of the machines when she was in her health food mood so there were no Sugar-Wackies or Hi Colas, but there *were* bags of peanuts and nut bars and fruit juices and so on, and one column of chocolate bars.

"So Eve called you," Faith said, examining

the machines to decide which one to give her large assortment of loose change. "Want a peanut bar?"

"Uh-huh. Dad told her I was coming to New York," Dana said.

"Well, that's interesting — that she called you, I mean."

"I guess so." Dana couldn't meet Faith's eyes.

"Come on, Dana. This is Faith."

"She invited me to a show on Saturday." Now Dana, her green eyes filled with mixed feelings, looked right at Faith.

"Is that what she did?" Faith asked.

"Yep."

"That's nice of her, Dana, you know." Faith tried to be reassuring. Dana didn't comment on Eve's niceness.

"I have my choice of *Take a Chance*, which is Off-Broadway and cute, the music sounds good. Or *Seven*, which is the big Broadway musical nobody else can get tickets for. Eve thought I might like *Take a Chance* better, but it's up to me entirely. Seems to me there are a lot of decisions these days that are up to me entirely." Dana sounded tired.

"You're not being fair," Faith said.

Dana laughed. "I know I'm not," she said. "It just so happens I do want to see *Take a Chance*, and Mom'll be busy Saturday afternoon. She works Saturdays, you know."

Faith was interested. "No, I didn't know. I

thought buyers . . . I don't know what I thought about buyers. Social workers, now, Saturday's not usually a workday."

"Well, Mom will be working, and my sister Maggie apparently has this big expedition to Hyde Park with her school class, so I may as well go to the show with Eve." Dana shrugged and tried to feel casual about the whole idea of an afternoon with Eve.

"I can't wait till Monday so you can tell me all about it," Faith said as they climbed the stairs back to their room. "Do you mind if I set the alarm for six tomorrow? I *have* to get Richie before he goes out to George's Diner to get a cheeseburger and French fries for breakfast. That's what I used to do," Faith said with a slightly embarrassed little smile. "He's into my old routine."

She stopped talking suddenly. Then she said, "Maybe when you come back, you'll have made up your mind about Hawaii. I'm not so sure I'm going to want to hear about *that*."

CHAPTER FIVE

Dana's boyfriend, Bret Harper, drove in his station wagon to Canby Hall from Oakley Prep, where he went to school. His car was very old and it rattled, and sometimes the horn stuck and blared for an hour at a time. Generally, though, it was reliable, and on Friday afternoon, Dana was very happy to see it arrive and hear it come to a noisy stop beside her just as she got to the front of Main Building at two-thirty. Bret was driving her to the station to catch her train home to New York.

"I'll pick you up the minute your last class is over," he had said the night before when they were making final arrangements.

"But listen," she had protested slightly. "You don't have to come by so early. My train doesn't leave till five-seventeen."

"Sure, I know," Bret had said, "but my mother always tells me to drive slowly."

Dana had laughed, but Bret had added

seriously, "It'll give us some time to talk about this thing."

That's why I love you, Bret, Dana had thought as she hung up. "You're a caring guy," she had said out loud while going up the stairs in the dorm just as Gloria Palmer was coming down. "I'm not a guy, I'm a girl," Gloria had answered, laughing at the startled expression on Dana's face.

When they were together in the car, and after they drove through the Canby Hall gates and made the left turn onto the road to town, Bret reached over and took Dana's hand. "Want to tell me more about it?" he asked gently.

Dana snuggled down against him, felt the strength of his arm under the worn smoothness of his jacket, felt his concern as a comforting presence. Preppy, funny Bret *was* a comfort! Instead of answering his question directly, she murmured something so softly he didn't hear her.

"Do you realize I almost didn't go to that school mixer at the beginning of the year and almost didn't meet you?" she said.

"Again, please," he said.

"I just said I'm glad you're here," Dana said, still softly.

"Sure. Okay. Now tell me all about it. From the beginning, Dana."

Dana straightened up and pushed back her hair. "You know most of it, Bret. About my dad and all and what he said."

"Your father's getting married again to this Eve person, and he wants you to come and live with them in Hawaii. I know that much. But tell me the hard parts," Bret answered.

"I'll tell you all the parts," Dana said. "I mean, it's very simple. I have to make a clear choice. I have to say yes or no to a really great invitation, and I seem to be the world's most confused girl because of it."

"You exaggerate," said Bret.

"I'm in a tailspin, Bret."

Bret put his right hand on top of her head and pretended to press down, although what he really did was ruffle her hair a little. "See, no more spinning," he said.

Dana laughed and turned toward her boyfriend. He grinned down at her now and said softly, "So start, Dana."

"Right. Well, it's just — you know. I don't know what to do. That's why I'm going home now. I don't want to make a decision like that. I want my mother to . . . I want to see my mother."

Bret was quiet, guiding the old car smoothly through the town traffic.

"Dana, you know what?" he said finally. "We both have a problem. I keep thinking how I don't want you to go away next year. I want you to be here." He kept looking straight ahead, but Dana felt as though he were looking right at her, looking lovingly into her eyes.

"Meeting you was the greatest thing that happened to me this year," he said. "I'd miss you more than I think I would, if you know what I mean, but to be fair, Hawaii can't be all bad either."

Dana put her head on his shoulder. "That just makes me go around in the same old circle."

He turned into the old train station and, without pausing, drove out of it again.

"Hey, we're here," Dana called out, looking over her shoulder as they left the station behind.

"We have an hour and a half," said Bret. "What do you say we go to the aquarium and look at the fish for a while?"

"Bret, no."

"What about the waterfront? We could say hello to the *Constitution*." The historic old ship was berthed at one of the docks there.

"Of course not," Dana protested.

"Ice cream?" he suggested.

"Yes."

He drove back to the station, where he parked, took her bag, and led her into a drugstore. Sitting on the old, curved wood benches of the Boston station, eating three-scoop ice-cream cones, they waited for the train. Bret put his arm around her.

"I think you'll feel better when you've seen your mother and all, Dana. I'll call you Monday and find out how it went." His voice was tight and he looked paler than usual.

"Okay. Right. And thanks, Bret." Dana smiled weakly.

He swung her bag over his shoulder, got on the train with her, saw her settled into a window seat, and went outside to wait, smiling and waving until the train hooted and started slowly to move away toward New York.

For Dana, it was odd but sensational to be in New York again with her mother and Maggie, the three of them snuggling together in the cab.

Now, with her floppy duffel under their feet, "How are you, old Mag?" Dana asked her sister, and, "Oh, Mom, it's great to see you," she added.

They went straight to their favorite delicatessen, around the corner from the apartment house where Dana had lived as long as she could remember, and had a late Friday supper: thick homemade soup and even thicker delicatessen sandwiches. For the girls, Friday had always meant no school tomorrow; for their mother, an end-of-week rest from planning meals. Dana had requested the deli dinner when they made the arrangements for her coming home.

They didn't talk much about her father's marriage and Eve's invitation to Dana, although it was hanging over them and they all knew it was a large part of the reason Dana was home. They referred to it briefly, but Dana somehow couldn't bring herself to get into the whole Hawaii thing that night.

Dana woke early Saturday morning. Canby Hall seemed a million miles from the New York-ness of being home, the coziness of the three of them together again.

She flopped into her mother's room and onto her mother's bed in her oversize T-shirt nightgown, her hair still tangled from sleep. Her mother came out of her bathroom, glistening, twisting a terrific blue-green silk scarf into the V-neck of her mauve sweater, zipping her skirt into place with practically the same motion.

"I must have been at West Point in another life," her mother said. "I must say I can get dressed faster than anybody else I know. Of course, it gives me that extra time . . . to hug my girl," and Dana got up for the hug.

"Mmm," Dana agreed.

"You really like Canby Hall, don't you, Dana? I mean, really," Carol Morrison asked.

"Yes, I really do, Mom. Shelley may drive me crazy before the year's over, but" — Dana hurried to reassure her mother — "she won't!"

They both laughed. The night before, Dana had regaled her mother and Maggie with an exaggerated report about Shelley's new career and her melodramatic struggle with having a crush on the town boy in the play and still being in love with her boyfriend back home.

There was certainly no time to talk to her mother this morning. It would have to wait.

The Off-Broadway theater where Dana was going to meet Eve was on 74th Street, way over east. She wanted very much to jog — her nerve endings seemed to be pleading for a run — but she knew she had to show up very smooth, very poised, very cool. She was wearing her favorite skirt and jacket. Maggie had sat cross-legged in front of her, looking up, head cocked, as she dressed. When she was ready, Maggie had approved. Okay — she wouldn't worry about her appearance.

As she waited for the light at the corner of 74th Street, knowing she was going to be early, Dana faced the fact that she felt like a baby. She had brought a book with her. If she was too early, if she had to wait around for Eve, she would just stand casually and catch up on some reading.

Dana couldn't imagine that Eve might be having a few qualms, too. She might have felt much easier if she had been able to be invisible in Eve's apartment and watch Eve dress with care, not too way-out, not too smart which was Dana's mother's style and false for Eve, but to be herself. Eve wanted to be at the theater at exactly the right moment, not too early but early enough.

Eve did not want Dana to have to wait for her. She would have preferred it the other way around, but as the taxi pulled up in front of the theater, there Dana was, absorbed in a book. Eve sat in the cab for a moment, until she realized the driver had been holding her change for quite a while.

"Lady!" he said in an exasperated voice.

"Sorry," Eve said.

She had been studying Dana, John's darling girl. Eve was glad John came, even part-time, with children.

Dana, sneaking a glance over the book, saw Eve in the cab. She had read the same paragraph four times; somehow she couldn't concentrate on the words. *That orange-yellow hair!*

"I hope you'll like this as much as I do," Eve said after the first strained hellos. Eve's hello had been a little ebulliant; Dana's a little extra-courteous.

"I'm sure it will be very nice," Dana said.

"When your father and I saw it, we —"

"You've seen it already?" Dana asked, surprised.

"Well, we both thought you'd like it, and I'm giving myself a treat, seeing it twice." Eve reached into her bag for the tickets.

Dana suddenly stopped being on best behavior, stopped being self-conscious. "Honestly, Eve? Really?"

"Honestly! I was excited by the dancers, by the way they move. You'll see what I mean," she said as she handed the tickets to the usher and they went into the theater.

It was a funny little theater, and it was

filling up, it seemed to Dana, with an awful lot of children. She suddenly felt as if she'd been doused with cold water. The show was obviously for children.

"There are a lot of tiny people here, aren't there?" she said with a slight edge to her voice.

Eve looked at her anxiously. Then she laughed. "Oh, because it's an afternoon performance. Anyway, it's a show, as they say, for children of all ages."

Dana wasn't sure she liked *that* comment. When the lights went down and the fanciful, colorful show began she tried to stay removed a bit. She cast small side glances at Eve, who was watching the stage with great enthusiasm as though she herself were a child. Eve leaned forward in her seat, a smile on her face as pantomimists performed their vivid movements, twisted and danced. Then Eve leaned back and cast a glance, in her turn, to Dana. Their eyes caught and Eve smiled. Dana did, too. She didn't know that her green eyes were telling Eve about the conflict she was feeling, the doubts she had, the way she was trying to resist being caught up in the play because enjoying it might represent disloyalty to her mother.

"I thought, since it's so early, you might like to come for a cup of tea at my apartment," Eve said as they left the theater.

"That would be nice," Dana answered hesitantly.

Dana felt as though she were made of hundreds of tiny antennae, all tuned to Eve and vibrating in different directions. Eve was so young. She was going to marry her father. Eve was sort of . . . *sound*, like Alison Cavanaugh. But so was her mother. Who needed Eve?!

Eve had a small loft in a building that was in a neighborhood that didn't seem to have apartments. When they came into the lobby, Dana realized that it was a beautiful building, with lots of marble and brass; it was elegant, Dana recognized that.

"It's an old landmark building," said Eve, fishing in her bag for her keys. "They've fixed it all up. I was lucky to get a place in it."

She opened her mailbox and quickly leafed through the contents, then made a funny, rueful face at Dana. Dana didn't understand at first, then she did: There wasn't a letter from her father. *How strange,* she thought. Her father wasn't just her father, somebody who mattered only to her and Maggie and had been part of her family. Her father was also the man Eve was in love with and waiting to hear from. Somehow that hurt Dana.

Dana was having a hard time putting her tumbling reactions into some kind of order.

"I hope tremendously that you'll come with us, Dana, that you'll make up your mind to," Eve said.

She filled a gleaming copper kettle with water and put it on the stove. A little table by a window was already set with cups, saucers, a plate of cookies, and a cake that Dana had a strong feeling Eve had made herself. Eve had prepared everything carefully, Dana realized. She had put a lot of attention into the afternoon.

"I come from a gigantic family," Eve said later, after she'd poured the tea and they both settled back. "My mother had four brothers and my father had two brothers and a sister, and we all lived within a couple of miles of each other. I was an only child, but you can imagine the number of cousins I had. And now most of *them* have children. That's almost the only thing I miss in New York, being surrounded by kids."

Dana couldn't imagine it. Eve seemed to her to be the total glamour woman. She hadn't thought Eve really wanted to have a child around. Not that she, Dana, was a child.

When Dana was leaving Eve's loft, Eve kissed her gently. "Let's be friends," Eve said shyly. "Please."

That night Maggie, Dana, and their mother went to the movies. When they got home Dana fell into bed, too tired to think about talking to her mother.

When Dana woke up on Sunday morning, she looked over at Maggie. Her sister was asleep, curled into a small bundle. One fist was clenched on her pillow. Dana always took Maggie for granted. She was the pesty little sister who had always been in the way. Now Dana realized that if she went to Hawaii, she wouldn't only be leaving Canby Hall and Faith and Shelley, not only her mother, but Maggie, too. Dana was surprised at the stab of pain that went through her at the thought.

She turned away from Maggie and thought about the time she had spent with Eve the day before. Eve was nice enough. She certainly was trying hard to get along with Dana, to please her, and be friendly. Dana didn't dislike Eve, but she hated the idea of Eve's marrying her father. Only her mother should be married to her father. Would she want to live with Eve for a year? To watch Eve and her father be a couple?

Dana stumbled out of bed and into the kitchen. She filled a bowl with granola and sliced an apple into it. She brushed back the long dark hair that fell into her face and tip-toed into her mother's room.

Carol Morrison was curled up almost exactly the way Maggie had been. Her hair, the same color as Dana's, though much shorter, was over her eyes. Dana peered down at her, trying to figure out if her mother was awake or just drifting, which her mother always told Dana was as important to her as sleeping. Dana carefully sat yoga-fashion on the bed and started chewing the granola as loudly as she could, hoping it would rouse her mother. Finally, Carol opened her eyes and said, "I hear you. I hear you." She smiled at Dana. "I'm glad you're here."

Dana put the bowl of cereal on a small table next to the bed and said softly. "I need help."

Carol Morrison sat up and pushed her hair behind her ears. "What kind of help?"

Dana stretched out and put her head in her mother's lap. "I know Dad told you about Hawaii. He said he had."

Her mother sighed cautiously. "Yes, he told me."

Dana sat up. "What should I do, Mom? I feel so confused." Her voice broke slightly.

Her mother looked away, and then back at her. "Dana, love, I can't decide this for you. I can't tell you what to do. You have to make up your own mind — all by yourself. If I pushed you one way or the other I'd feel guilty."

Dana flopped down on the bed again and looked up at her mother. "I want to go, Mom. It's exciting, the idea of going to live in a strange place. Mom, it's why I came home ... to talk to you."

Carol Morrison's face was expressionless.

Dana went on. "But I don't want to leave Canby Hall. I don't want to leave *you*."

Carol's face remained still, but Dana was sure she saw a flicker of happiness in her eyes. At that moment, her mother stood up and reached for her robe. "Dana, dear, I won't tell you what to do. But sometimes when I can't make up my mind about something, can't make a choice, I take a piece of paper and in one column I write all the good things about the choice and in another column I write all the bad things. Then I just see which outweighs the other — the good or the bad."

Dana turned onto her side and was surprised to feel a tear running down her cheek. "No fifteen-year-old should have to make a decision like this."

Her mother laughed. "I guess fifteen is as good a time as any to start really growing up. But I know it's hard. I do." She leaned down and kissed Dana gently. "Please try to understand, I can't help you much with this. It's not fair to ask me."

When, finally, Dana was on the train going back to Canby Hall, she realized she was almost more troubled than she had been since her father had first presented the idea of her going to Hawaii with him and Eve. There was no question now that Eve was nice, that Eve wanted her to come with them, that Hawaii would be terrific, that it would be wonderful to be with her father again. There was no question, either, that she still wanted her father to be married to her mother and only her mother. Dana felt a tremendous alliance with her mother. If she went with her dad and Eve, wouldn't she be betraying her?

Dana leaned her head against the back of her seat and felt that it was all too much. She didn't have any better an idea what she should do than she had had when she came home to New York. If only her mother had simply *told* her what to do. Dana wasn't sure this business of growing up, of having to make life-changing decisions for herself, was all so wonderful. She wasn't sure it was something she wanted anymore.

CHAPTER SIX

Tom Stevenson, Shelley explained to Dana and Faith, was the best-looking boy she had ever seen in her life, including, she had to confess, Paul. Tom had hair that was so black it looked blue sometimes.

"Did you ever see hair that black?" she demanded of them.

"Shelley," Faith answered. "*I've* seen lots of black hair."

"Oh, you know what I mean," Shelley said. "And his voice. Well, of course his voice has to be fantastic because he's going to be an actor. I mean, I think he is. He's already a very fine actor, really. Anyway, very good. There's a line he has . . . well, I won't bore you with the actual script, but when Tom read it today in rehearsal, instead of stressing the word *going*, the way I thought he would, he stressed *will you* so that the whole sense was altered, and yet it was —"

"I see," Faith said dutifully.

"He seriously wants to be an actor. He's been in school plays, at his own school, since he was a freshman. Did I tell you he plays the trumpet? Isn't that fascinating? He's also applying to the drama department of Carnegie-Mellon University, the best undergraduate drama department in the whole country. I just wonder whether that might be a good college for me to go to? No, I'm not even going to think about it now. I'll think about the play, about rehearsals. What's today? Wednesday. There isn't another rehearsal until Friday, but Tom and I are going to go through our lines together . . ."

Dana was exasperated. What difference did it make when they were going to rehearse? What *real* difference did it make that Shelley had a crush on Tom? Dana was the one with the *important* decision to make.

"You must promise to tell us every little thing about it," Dana said. "You won't forget. Everything! How he got up and how he sat down and how he wiggled his left toe. Promise?"

Shelley stopped short, her mouth open in surprise and hurt.

"Dana?" she said hesitantly. After a pause, she asked, "Dana, aren't you interested in whether or not I —"

"Interested? Why, Shelley, spelled S-h-e-l-l-e, Hyde, spelled as usual —"

"Can it, Dana," Faith said, feeling frightened suddenly.

"I don't know what she's talking about. I'm *breathless* with interest in Tom," Dana continued.

"Yeah?" Faith said.

Dana turned back to her books and Shelley, tossing her head with an attempt at disdain, started to pace back and forth in the room. She walked catty-corner to avoid stepping on Faith's shoes, the wastebasket in the middle of the room, the plastic laundry basket filled with Faith's neatly folded clean laundry (also in the middle of the room) and six drawers of Dana's bureau, all of which were open and jutting out. Although the girls had a triple, the room could barely contain Shelley's dramatic stride. Every time she passed Dana, she either brushed against her chair or swirled and ruffled Dana's papers. Faith, at her desk at the other end of the room, looked on with her quizzical smile as Shelley swooped by Dana. Dana clenched her teeth and flattened her papers, looked heavenward.

"The terrible problem," Shelley exclaimed, "is how will I tell Paul that I am going to be an actress after I finish school? Poor Paul. He'll be so upset. He thinks I'm coming right home."

"Shelley, will you knock it off, please?" Dana said quietly.

"But don't you understand I've changed the entire course of my life?" Shelley said dramatically.

"The course of *your* life," Dana said angrily. "What about mine? I may *really* have to change my life."

Dana threw herself on her bed. "Why don't you just forget the course of your life for a while and concentrate on a schoolbook. You're in school, you know. Since you discovered you were Duse, you —"

"Who?"

Dana sat up and glared at Shelley. "She was a great immortal actress, like Sarah Bernhardt. You probably never even heard of Bernhardt."

Shelley burst into tears. "I *did*," she cried. "What's wrong with you, Dana?"

Suddenly, standing stock-still in the middle of the room, her stomach out, head bent, Shelley turned into a little girl.

Dana exploded again. "I don't know! I'm going to the library." She slammed out of the room before Faith could stop her.

"Wow," said Faith. "Come on, Shel. Don't cry. Dana's just very upset. You can be sure she really cares about you."

"I don't know about that," Shelley said in between sobs.

When Dana came back from the library that night she didn't say good night to either roommate. In the morning, she made a point of leaving Baker House early to have breakfast alone, but Faith ran after her.

"Dana, what's with you?"

"Faith, you know it's not you. I just can't

take little Shelley anymore. Oh, Paul," Dana
mimicked. "Oh, Tom. Oh, Pine Bluff, Iowa.
It's all so *dumb!*"

Dana stopped walking and brushed at the
tears running down her cheeks. Her voice
shook.

"Shelley makes such a big number out of
nothing, while I literally have to decide where
and how and with whom I am going to live
a couple of months from now. I mean, going
to *live.* Do I want to go five thousand miles
away, and not come back here, and leave my
mother and you and even Shelley and Canby
Hall? Or do I want to be with my father in
Hawaii with a new wife? I'm just going nuts
with it all, Faith, and until I decide what to
do, I don't care about Shelley's tiny troubles."

Dana slipped her arm through Faith's.
"Really, Faith, I'm *scared.*"

"I know," Faith said, "but I hate to see you
and Shelley fighting. She doesn't mean to be
thoughtless — or boring."

"I know," Dana said, "and I hate being so
mean to her. She's getting on my nerves, but
it'll be okay."

"I sure hope so," Faith said.

"So do I," said Dana softly as they parted
— Dana to the Science Building for first-
period chemistry and Faith to Main Building
for American history.

CHAPTER SEVEN

Shelley knew about being in love. She and Paul been going steady since early high school days. They'd confided in each other, shared each other's joys and sorrows, stood with their arms around each other watching sunrises together on golden Iowa mornings. All through freshman year in high school, they had declared their love and thought of themselves as an ideal couple.

Why, then, Shelley wondered as she sat at the round table with Tom, Sue Barlow, John Whitticomb from Oakley, and Anne Prior, who was the stage manager, *do I feel the way I do about Tom?*

They had all just gotten their notes from Ms. Mac and were sharing the last few minutes before the rehearsal broke up and they had to go out once again into their everyday school world.

Tom was leaning back in his chair, one arm slung around the back of the chair, the other loose, flying in the air as he told a funny story. Shelley almost didn't hear the words. She was lost in admiration of the tone of his voice. She thought it was the most beautiful male voice she had ever heard, that his New England accent made everything he said even more wonderful to listen to.

Shelley felt she had never known a boy as handsome or as dynamic as Tom, or as serious, yet at the same time humorous. The fact that she was in the same room with him, sharing the same table, sitting directly opposite him, was exciting to her.

Then something even more exciting happened. Shelley heard Tom say something to somebody about never having been around the Canby Hall campus.

"You mean you haven't had the grand tour?" Shelley asked him, not even aware of having burst in on a conversation.

"Nope," said Tom. "I've only seen what I can see from my bike, coming to rehearsals."

"We'll have to do something about that," Shelley said. "Would you like a tour?"

"Sure," said Tom, and then and there they made a date. After the rehearsal, Shelley would show Tom the Canby Hall campus. *What if Paul knew?* Shelley thought.

The wonderful, excited feeling stayed with her as the group around the round table got up, left the library, and went out into the afternoon air. Shelley could feel an uncontrollable blush warming her face — she wished she didn't blush so easily — when John asked, "Coming into town, Tom? I can give you a ride."

"No," Tom said, "thanks anyway. I'm sticking around."

John left for his car, and Shelley hoped Sue and Anne would go away, too, but they didn't. Tom smiled at all three girls, very smoothly, Shelley thought. Then he said, "Shelley is going to show me around your school. Where do you think we ought to start?"

"The tennis court," Sue answered immediately.

"The barn and stable," Anne said at the same time.

"I thought the wishing pond," said Shelley in a dreamy voice.

They all laughed, Shelley not quite as heartily as the others.

They strolled toward the park directly in front of them, which was the center of the Canby Hall campus. As they got to the wishing pond, Sue noticed the look on Shelley's usually open and cheerful Midwestern face. Her expression pleaded with Sue, begged Sue to understand that Shelley wanted to be alone with Tom.

"I'm going to the language lab," Sue said and disappeared.

Anne may or may not have seen the same expression. A senior and an efficient girl who took her responsibilities as stage manager of the spring play very seriously, Anne suddenly realized that she had left her script behind.

"My script," she cried and ran back to the library.

"*Now* we are alone," said Tom dramatically with a little crooked smile that struck Shelley like a beam of sunshine. With Paul, Shelley knew she would just have laughed at the line. She would have put her arm through Paul's and said, "Yes, you and me. And *this* is the wishing pond. I don't know if you can see them now, but it's stocked with golden carp. When you fed them, they come right up to the surface."

But she wasn't with Paul, and she didn't feel comfortable.

"This is the wishing pond," she said in a voice that, to her astonishment, was shaky. She laughed in embarrassment. "Sometimes girls throw things in there when they need good luck for a test. I mean, money. They throw in pennies."

"Gross," said Tom cheerfully.

"Yes," said Shelley. "Well, yes," she said again. "Um, if you look straight ahead, you'll see my dorm, and then if you look to the right, you'll see the maple groves. All those are maple trees. We tap maple syrup at Canby Hall. I mean, *I* don't tap maple syrup, but it gets tapped from those trees."

Tom seemed to be looking everywhere,

watching the girls streaming from Main Building, Science Building, and the library, and gathering around their dorms. On pretty days like this, clusters of girls often sat out on the dormitory lawns. In front of Baker House, Shelley noticed, there were several groups of girls talking together. *They look like a bouquet of flowers*, she thought in amazement and glanced up at Tom. Did he think things like that, too?

"Over here," she said, turning and starting to walk away from the dorms toward the barn and the farmhouse. "Over here is what Canby Hall was like before it was Canby Hall."

Tom laughed, and suddenly Shelley felt at least a twinge more confidence than she had felt ten minutes earlier.

"What I mean is that the original Canby Hall was an estate with a big house, but it was also a working farm and the school has kept all these original farm buildings."

They walked through the barn, which had in it the dozen horses that were kept for the girls who rode.

"Do you do much horseback riding?" Tom asked Shelley.

"No, not here," Shelley answered. "I used to at home. We live in town, but lots of my friends live on farms outside of town, and I've spent some time riding their horses."

Tom approached one of the horses in one

of the stalls, palm up so the horse could sniff it. Tom then gently turned his hand and patted the horse's nose.

They left the barn and ambled more easily across the campus.

"If I'm going to give you a real tour," Shelley said, "I should have started with Canby Hall's history. Have you ever heard of Horace Canby? About a hundred years ago he was a big industrialist. He had a daughter named Julia, and Julia died in Europe when she was twelve. Horace Canby made a girls' school on this estate, which would have belonged to Julia Canby if she had lived."

Tom smiled down at Shelley, and tossed his scarf around his neck and over his shoulders. It was a long, thin wool scarf that Shelley could not imagine Paul wearing or, if he did wear one like it, flinging it as casually, as dramatically as Tom had done.

"I've lived in this town all my life," he said, "and this school's been here all the time, but I didn't know that's how it came to be a school."

"Yes," said Shelley. "And you know what else? The school mascot is a lioness."

By now they were approaching the birch grove and stopping in front of the statue of a lioness with her cubs. It was an old-fashioned-looking bronze statue. "GIFT OF THE CLASS OF 1917, IN HONOR OF THE TWENTIETH ANNIVERSARY OF THE FOUNDING OF CANBY HALL," read a bronze plaque on the stone base.

"There's a saying that the milk of the lioness is so precious and so powerful that if you put it in an ordinary cup, the cup breaks," said Shelley.

"Wow," said Tom, turning abruptly to look down at her.

Shelley added, "Everytime anybody breaks a cup in the dining hall, everybody yells out, 'so precious and so powerful!' "

Tom was quiet.

"Oh, it's just a joke," said Shelley. "I think it's pretty dumb." She paused. "Well, I guess that's the tour. I mean, we could walk for miles more if you wanted to. But I don't think you're particularly interested in seeing the power plant, are you?"

"I'd love to see the power plant," he said, "but maybe some other time?"

"Sure," Shelley said.

As Shelley walked toward the parking lot alongside Tom, she felt like crying. They had been alone together, and she had acted so dumb and silly he would probably never want to spend any time with her again. Could he tell she thought he was wonderful? Did he know that she really wasn't as dopey as she seemed? For a clear moment, Shelley thought of her two older brothers and how, facing their teasing and their demands, she had always managed to come across with confidence and strength.

"Oh, boy!" she said emphatically.

Tom, startled, looked down at her.

"I just realized how very far from Iowa I am at this moment," she said.

Tom stopped walking, put his finger under Shelley's chin, lifted her face so that they could look directly at each other, and said, "Listen, Shelley, are you ever allowed off this place? How would you like a small tour of town on Saturday?"

Shelley didn't quite trust her voice, so she just nodded, very enthusiastically.

"That's great," said Tom. "We've got a date?" She nodded again. As though in one motion, Tom took his bicycle from the rack, got on, waved, and headed for the great wrought-iron gateway of Canby Hall. Before he disappeared, he took his hands from the handlebars and, without looking back, wiggled them both in the air in a gesture of farewell. Shelley thought it was terrific. She wanted to race to Room 407 and report the fantastic events of the past hour to her roommates.

CHAPTER EIGHT

The next day during Study Hours things were almost the same — or worse. At eight in the evening, the girls in 407 were doing what they were supposed to be doing: working quietly at their desks. Dana had pushed her problem to the back of her head for a while and was applying herself whole-heartedly to translating a page of Latin. One of the astonishing facts of her life at Canby Hall, possibly the most surprising to Dana, was her taking Latin — and liking it. Even though she had read about Latin courses in the school catalogue, she hadn't believed it; it had sounded too much like the Dark Ages, when her *grandparents* went to school. But, as she reported in amazement to her mother and even to selected friends at home, she discovered she not only took Latin, but she liked it.

She was bent over, writing in her notebook, her bare feet curled around the legs of her chair.

Faith was leaning back in her desk chair, her long legs in sweat pants, her feet in sneakers up on her desk, and her book open on her lap. It had taken Shelley, even Dana, some time to accept the fact that their lanky roommate actually felt comfortable studying in that position and never, so far as they knew, toppled over backward while doing it.

Dana's pencil moved, paused, tapped, and wrote again on the page in her notebook. Faith turned pages. Shelley was the only one absolutely still. She had pushed away the list of French idioms she had been trying to cram into her head and now was staring down, frozen, at the pink notepaper in front of her and at her hand holding a purple felt-tip pen.

"Oh, I can't!" she finally cried out.

Faith's legs came down with a crash. Dana jumped.

"What happened?" Faith asked.

"What's wrong?" Dana called out.

"I can't write to Paul. I don't know what to say to him. I can't break his heart," Shelley exclaimed.

There was an instant of dead silence.

"Did you make that noise about *that*?" Dana demanded. Faith simply dropped her forehead to her desk and covered her head with her arm.

"Why *won't* you understand, Dana?" Shelley asked.

"Well, I'll tell you," Dana began, swiveling in her chair, "you've become —"

"Dana! Shelley! Don't —" Faith began.

Suddenly their rising voices were overwhelmingly drowned out by the piercing scream of the fire alarm.

"Another dumb fire drill," Dana said. "Would you believe?"

Faith dashed to the door, opened it briefly, then closed it.

"Fire drill nothing. There's smoke out in that hall, children."

The girls knew what to do. Shelley grabbed a blanket, Dana her coat and handbag, and Faith her camera. Then they cautiously opened the door again. Looking out, they saw other girls moving swiftly to the fire stairs. The three girls left the room, closed the door, and made for the fire stairs, trying not to knock into each other or the others.

Jackie Adams was giggling. "I think I'm getting hysterical," she said. "Does anybody know what happened?"

"What happened?" Joan Barr kept asking.

All the girls kept walking as they had done in fire drills. But there was a difference, a restless hurrying. Dana was struggling into her coat as she moved; Shelley was wrapping the blanket around her frilly pink cotton robe; Faith was holding her camera carefully while she, too, moved as fast as she could. They had had lots of fire drills, but this alarm was so loud! It didn't stop! They could smell smoke! They could hear sirens now. The fire engines from town were coming.

The Baker House girls gathered across the road in the park, and Alison immediately started roll call. "Joan? Faith? Jackie?"

"Okay," said Alison. Faith had noticed she took a very deep breath after roll call, but Alison was trying to act as though a real fire emptying Baker House quickly was a casual matter.

"Okay, girls," she said again, gesturing to them to cluster together. "All present and accounted for."

She glanced over her shoulder toward the house where two large fire engines were parked, as the volunteer firemen in business suits, work clothes, and one man in pajamas and bathrobe, swarmed all over, hatchets handy, hoses strung out, rubber boots stomping into Baker.

The area was swarming with other people, too. Addison House and Charles House, the dorms on each side of Baker, had emptied, too, and like Alison, the houseparents from the other dorms were calling roll and assembling their girls. Poor Mrs. Franklin in Charles House carried her babies: a three-year-old and an infant. She had tucked her little boy under her arm, where he was screaming, and the infant in a canvas sack on her back was also screaming. Everyone on the whole campus had dashed to where the noise was coming from, and administration people were all trying to keep the girls away from the fire trucks, trying to avoid an incipient panic.

From the moment it looked as though everyone was safe and their dorm wouldn't come tumbling down, Faith concentrated on taking pictures. Alison had her arms around one of the younger girls in the dorm, a freshman whose face was like an *O* of wonderment. Through her camera, Faith saw Alison in her comforting pose, the surprised girl, a fire engine directly behind them and focused carefully. A news photographer had to be able to make quick decisions about what was news, what told a story. Snap, and she had the picture. Faith looked around. She wanted to get the firemen in pajamas, and Mrs. Franklin, the houseparent from Charles House, juggling her babies and her dorm girls, and ...

"Okay," Alison said a third time. "I think it's getting a little cool out here. Let's move to the dining hall until the firemen tell us it's safe to go back."

The girls began to leave the park reluctantly, because nobody wanted to miss any of the excitement. But the night air, even though spring was coming, still had a chill in it and not everyone had been as smart as Shelley with her blanket or Dana with her coat. There was a mass movement toward the dining hall.

It had been a minor fire. Marilyn Ryan, the only Baker House girl who had come out of the dorm hysterical, had been smoking — "Forbidden, as we all know," Alison said much later — and somehow had dropped a lit cigarette into her wastebasket. The basket had burst into flames and ignited the synthetic drapes, which made more smoke than anyone dreamed possible. It had been taken care of almost immediately, and the girls in Charles House and Addison House were already back in their dorms when Alison announced that the smoke was still heavy in Baker. For tonight, the Baker House girls would split up and go to the other two dorms. There would be some doubling up, but it would just be for the one night. Tomorrow everything would be all right again.

Half the Baker girls, including Shelley, Dana, and Faith, were assigned to Addison House. They went over in a group and were greeted by the houseparents, Mr. and Mrs. Druyan. As they sat around in the Addison House lounge, it seemed odd but nice that there was a husband and wife team of houseparents.

The girls were past the excitement of the fire and feeling weary. Still, they noticed that Addison House, which was the newest of the three dormitories, was much sleeker than their own dorm.

Cheerful, Dana thought, with its bright

red, straight-line sofas and tan egg-shell plastic chairs, which were in fact very comfortable. Baker's lounge was entirely different. It looked more like an old-fashioned, comfortable living room, with overstuffed sofas and an Oriental rug on the floor, but then Baker House had been one of the houses on the grounds when the school first opened a hundred years earlier. Addison House had been built much later.

Dana was sitting next to Faith. On the other side of her was a girl she really knew only to say hi to. The girl immediately put out her hand. As Dana extended her own hand, the girl said, "Nancy Plummer. I'm glad to meet someone who can put colors together as terrifically as you did yesterday. You wore a blue-green scarf and a mauve sweater."

Dana laughed, the first easy laugh she'd had almost since her dad's visit and his invitation to Hawaii. "How'd you remember?"

"Color is my life's work. I'm majoring in art."

Dana laughed again. "Dana Morrison," she said. "I wish I could take credit for the combination, but my mother's a fashion buyer; she put them together."

"Lucky you. My mother's a doctor. Her clothes sense runs to white coat over everything. Listen, as long as there's going to be room-sharing, would you like to share mine?"

It was all right with the Druyans, and soon Nancy was showing Dana some Addison House rooms.

"You see," she said, "my single is really connected on both sides to other singles. All the rooms are like that, so if you want to be a *single* single, you just close your door and you're alone. But if you want to share, well, you just open the door — and presto — roommate!"

"That sounds great," said Dana. "I have a roommate at the moment I would love to close the door on."

"Poor you," said Nancy. "That must be tough."

"Well, she's a nice girl, of course . . ."

Nancy laughed. "Of course. Except some of the world's nicest girls are the world's greatest pains in the neck."

Dana was silent. She felt a sharp sense of disloyalty talking like that about Shelley to this virtual stranger.

"Maybe. Sometimes," she murmured. "Um, what do you mean, you're majoring in art?"

"Oh, I like to paint."

Dana looked around the walls of the room a little more carefully than she had when she came in. "Are these yours?" she asked, going to a cluster of blotchy, vibrant watercolors that had been tacked to the wall with push pins.

"They are," Nancy said.

"I like them," Dana said. "They remind me

of . . ." She wasn't even aware of how deeply she sighed as she interrupted herself.

"Hey, that sounded very heavy."

"What did?" Dana asked.

"Well, you were looking at my stuff and then you sighed such a deep sigh. I hate to think they bothered you *that* much."

"Did I sigh?" Dana asked. "Well, I guess your pictures, your colors, reminded me of Hawaii."

"Hawaii?" Nancy said. "You've been there?"

Dana flopped down on a bean-bag chair and stretched her legs out in front of her. "No, I've never been there. The big question is, am I going? It's very long and involved." Dana glanced over at Nancy Plummer, whom she knew only slightly, and saw an alert, sensitive intelligence in the girl's brown eyes and vitality in the way she sat on the floor hugging her knees, her face sympathetic.

"Well, the thing is," Dana began, and told her story. ". . . and they want me to come with them —"

"For a year?" Nancy interrupted.

"Yes, for the whole time they're there."

Nancy whistled a little. "That's really a problem," she said. "What do you think you're going to do?"

Dana ran her hand through her hair. "If I only knew!" she said. "I mean, what girl in her right mind would give up the chance to spend a year in Hawaii? Right?"

"Hmm, well . . ." Nancy said.

"My dad's been away for a long time now," Dana said. "I mean, I haven't lived with him since he moved out, and he's such a great guy. It would be wonderful to be with him again."

Nancy nodded. "Oh, I understand that. My folks are divorced, too, but they have been for so long, I almost can't remember when they were together."

"Did your father get married again?" Dana asked.

"My folks are *both* remarried," Nancy said. "It's okay. My dad's wife — she's sort of a country club person. You know, they both play golf a lot. It's kind of nice. My mother's a doctor; her husband Fred's a doctor, too. They're both very busy all the time — no golf! I live with my mom and Fred. Then summers, long holidays when I want to, and weekends, I go stay with Dad and Peggy. That's the way it's been for me, almost since I can remember."

"I can't get used to the idea of my dad with another wife," Dana said softly.

Nancy said matter-of-factly, "I can't imagine any other way. Listen," she said almost as an afterthought, "if you go to Hawaii for the whole year, you won't be coming back to school."

"I *know*," Dana said.

"I kind of like it here. Don't you?"

"I do," Dana said, "I really do."

"Even when they have fires?" Nancy said

with a grin. "Wasn't that really something? I think the way everyone cleared out so fast and safely and how the whole thing went shows that we really are a pack of lionesses."

Dana laughed. "Sure we are."

"Do you know how it started?" Nancy asked, and Dana began to tell her. They went on talking easily and comfortably until there was a knock on the door and Mrs. Druyan suggested that they turn out their lights and go to sleep.

CHAPTER NINE

Somehow in the next few weeks, Dana, Shelley, and Faith, who had been such close friends, best friends, seemed to be going their separate ways more often. After classes, they didn't see much of each other anymore, and even when they did, it wasn't very satisfying.

On Monday, Dana went to her extracurricular activity right after last period English without stopping in front of the big TV at the Student Center, as all three girls had done almost every day of their life at Canby Hall. They *had* to see at least one soap opera before going to their afterclass activities. Faith and Shelley waited for Dana through most of *Rage for Life* but then gave up.

"I guess she didn't want to get yelled at again for being late to choir," Shelley said, avoiding Faith's eyes.

"Sure, that's it," Faith agreed, but she didn't look directly at Shelley either.

They both knew Dana's choir group met on Wednesday. Mondays she went to Latin Club, which was much more informal about everything, including promptness. Latin Club was a group of eight girls who, like Dana, had discovered they enjoyed learning the old language. Defending their somewhat quirky choice of an extracurricular activity, some of the Latin Club girls said it was because Latin helped your English, and the better your English, the higher your S.A.T. scores. Others considered it a terrific status symbol. All of them thought it was a little exotic.

When Faith and Shelley parted for their own activities, Faith going to the *Clarion*, Shelley to the spring play rehearsal, they both felt off-center. With Dana absent from their ritual, something was missing. It was like not saying hi in the morning or bye when they separated. Both girls felt the difference and reacted.

When she got to the *Clarion* office, Faith flung her camera case onto the battered old desk, and after Grace Barish said, "Quiet, please. I'm trying to get this column finished," Faith was surprised at the surge of anger she felt. She caught herself in time. "Sorry, Gracie," she said.

Shelley was upset, too. She got mad at Tom because he didn't break off his conversation with a couple of the other actors the instant she came into the Round Table Room.

* * *

Dana didn't seem to notice, or acknowl-
edge, any change in her relationship with
her roommates. It seemed to her that she was
just becoming more comfortable with her
new friend Nancy, who didn't think much of
soap operas. So Dana wasn't watching them
much anymore.

"One day I cut all my afternoon classes
and spent the whole time right *there*, watching soaps," Dana confessed to Nancy, point-
ing toward a bench facing the Student Center's large TV.

Nancy put her index finger to her mouth
and puffed out her cheeks. "Barf," she said.

"Yes, I guess so," Dana said in regretful
agreement.

In the few weeks since they had met, Dana
and Nancy had become good friends. Part of
the reason was that Nancy understood so
much of Dana's problem because her own
parents were divorced, remarried, and living
in different places. It turned out that Nancy
often had to make a choice similar to Dana's.
They got along in other areas, too, even areas
where there might have been disagreement.
Nancy avoided all forms of exercise, even
compulsory school sports. She thought Dana's
jogging around the campus "in circles," as
she put it, was an astonishing waste of time
and energy.

"Anyway, the way to go around and around
this place is slowly," Nancy said once. "Then
you can really look at the colors."

"I look when I run," Dana said. "Don't you think I know there are pale green buds on the trees?" Both girls laughed.

They had come into the Student Center to get some sandwiches at the vending machines; there was more than an hour to go before dinner. After the snack they were going over to the Language Lab to listen to tapes for a while. Dana had a question-and-answer vocabulary tape to study for her Spanish class, and Nancy, in third-year French, had a short essay to hear and understand.

"I wish this was a pizza," Nancy said, biting into a thin ham-and-cheese sandwich. "Want a Tab?"

"Yeah, sure," said Dana. "No, wait." She had just seen Faith come in, camera slung over her shoulder, carrying a handful of papers that she waved at Dana. "I think Faith's got my mail. She sometimes gets it for Shelley and me when she passes the mailroom. Be back in a second."

Dana crossed the lounge to meet Faith.

"Great pickings today," Faith said. "Two real letters and the L.L. Bean catalogue."

Dana took her mail. "Thanks loads. Oh, look. This one's from Bret." Dana opened the big white envelope. "Hey, it's an invitation to the opening of Oakley Prep's Photography Exhibit."

"Yes, I know," said Faith gloomily. "I got one, too."

"From Ray Dixon?" asked Dana, looking at Faith with a question in her eye.

"Who else?" Faith answered.

"I don't know why you're so set against poor Raymond. Just because he likes you," said Dana.

"He doesn't even know me," Faith answered. "We met exactly once, and he was so anxious to show me what a great camera he had and what a great photographer he was, he jammed the thing and had to use *my* pictures for *his* story."

"Well, that's what I mean. You're both photographers for your school papers, and Oakley and Canby Hall are practically sister-brother schools, and he's smart, he's handsome, his clothes are terrific —"

"Dana!" Faith interrupted.

"Sorry. You know me. I like clothes," Dana said.

"Okay. I'll finish it for you. He's also rich, black — and too preppy for this girl."

"Oh, *Faith*," Dana groaned. "But you can go to the opening of the exhibit, can't you?"

"Maybe," Faith said, still not cheery.

Dana glanced at the Hawaiian return address on her other letter and put it into her pocket unopened.

"From my dad," she explained sheepishly. "I'll look at it later." She started to stare into space. "You know what, Faith. When I woke up this morning, I decided definitely that I was going to Hawaii with Dad and Eve. It was absolutely definite. Then here comes this letter and I start thinking about my Mom and how I don't want to be so far away from her, or be disloyal to her, and now I'm not sure again."

"Back to square one, right?" Faith said. Dana nodded.

At one corner of the room, someone was playing the Jane Fonda exercise tape.

"Right," Dana said, and began to walk toward the action around the tape. Suddenly she wanted some physical activity.

Faith noticed that Shelley was among the girls exercising and wondered if Dana noticed it, too. Faith was worried and stood for a moment, watching both girls. There were about five or six girls in the corner of the room, giving each other space enough to move, to lie on the floor and kick, to bend without bumping into anyone. Faith saw that Shelley, aware of Dana's approach, was trying to look unconcerned, doing the exercises a little more vigorously than she had been doing them before. Faith moved to the vending machine, greeted Nancy casually, bought herself peanut-butter crackers, and continued her observation of her roommates.

Dana, who kept particularly fit with her jogging and by the exercises she practiced before and after she ran, seemed absorbed in obeying everything Jane Fonda's disembodied voice called out. Her long hair fell over her face as she bent forward, flew behind her as she turned to the right and to the left. Faith slumped in her chair; her roommates were not talking to each other. *This is getting serious,* she thought. Something had to be done, but she didn't know what.

Nancy, finishing the last of her second sandwich and Tab, said good-bye to Faith and walked over toward the exercisers.

"Hey, Dana . . ." she called out.

Dana stopped exercising and pushed her hair back. "I was just working out a kink or two. I'm ready to go." Faith returned Dana's wave as she and Nancy, hoisting their handbags and books, left the Student Center for the Language Lab.

Faith was angry at Dana. How could she ignore Shelley, who continued the exercises vigorously, too vigorously; then, as though she were a windup toy running down, slowly began to move out of time. Finally she stopped.

"It doesn't matter," she said to Faith, who came over. "Tom likes me the way I am. He says I'm pleasingly plump."

"Good for Tom," Faith said.

Faith, seeing the hurt look on Shelley's face, realized that for her own sake and for the sake of her roommates, whom she knew really cared about each other, she was going to have to do something to bring them together again. She couldn't lock them in a room until they made up. She didn't want to run to Alison. Faith couldn't think of any-

thing cute — or sensible, either — that she
believed would work. The only person she
could think of who would not only understand the situation, but come up with a solu-
tion, was her mother. Faith was sure that if
her mother applied some of her social worker
art to the split between Dana and Shelley,
everything would be all right. But her mother
was too far away and too busy at work to
come to Canby Hall. No amount of wishing
could bring her here. *Well*, Faith thought, *if
Mother can't come to Canby Hall, maybe I
ought to take some of Canby Hall to her.*

Faith sat upright in her chair. That was
what she was going to do. She was going to
invite Dana and Shelley to come home to
Washington with her for a weekend. If anybody in the world could reconcile her friends,
Faith was sure that person was her mother.

CHAPTER TEN

Ｎone of the three girls, even Faith, really believed it was happening, but there they were Friday morning on the plane to New York, ready to make the quick switch at Kennedy Airport to fly the rest of the way to Washington for the weekend. Although they hadn't been able to get seats together — Shelley and Faith were sitting next to each other on the window side and Dana was across from them — they *were* together. This was the first time they had been a trio in a completely social way since the fire. The politeness between them was almost overwhelming, though, and Faith felt the knot of apprehension at the top of her head slide all the way down to her toes. She hoped this great idea of hers was going to work.

As though reading Faith's thoughts, Dana leaned across the aisle and said, "It's a blast, Faith," and Shelley nodded in agreement.

"I almost can't believe it," Shelley said. "Washington, D.C., the nation's capital." But as she continued, Dana closed her eyes in exasperation and Faith smiled almost desperately.

"I'm doing so many things no one in Iowa would believe," Shelley said.

Faith and Dana knew what she meant. Shelley was thinking about Tom and Paul. Both her roommates waited for Shelley's dramatic speech about the effect her wanting to be an actress — and her feelings for Tom — would have on her family and Paul at home in Iowa. It was what Dana now called "the performance." Dana leaned back in her seat, trying not to listen — not to notice Shelley's sighs and tiny groans.

It was really curious, Dana reflected, how Shelley's carrying on about the theater and about Tom and Paul, always seemed to make her, Dana, more confused about her own situation. Sometimes Dana felt she had it under control, that she could really list all the elements in her problem and look at them sensibly enough to come to a decision. But whenever Shelley started "the performance," Dana's calm disintegrated and her lists went swirling away.

Dana reached for the airline magazine in the pocket in front of her seat. She could hear Shelley now talking excitedly about visiting Washington. "My father said I have to see the

Declaration of Independence," she said. Dana
was torn two ways. She wanted to join the
conversation. She was excited about the
weekend, too. It would be nice to slide back
into the harmony the three roommates always used to have. But Dana was afraid that
Shelley would upset her, so she turned instead to the puzzle page of the magazine.

The entire Thompson family was at the
airport to meet the girls. When they walked
into the waiting room, Sarah rushed up to her
Faith and hugged her tightly. Richie hung
back, trying to look uninvolved, but the
smile on his face was proof of his pleasure
in having Faith home. Joan Thompson,
Faith's mother, waited until Sarah had let go
and then she took Faith in her arms and
held her. She finally pushed the girl away
and said, "Let me look at you."

She carefully examined Faith from top to
bottom and then declared, "You've lost weight.
You're working too hard."

Faith laughed and pulled her mother toward Dana and Shelley. Joan Thompson
looked at the girls in the same careful way
she did Faith. She took Dana's hand and
squeezed it. "Obviously, you are Dana." Then
she turned to Shelley. "And you're Michelle
— Shelley — without a doubt."

Dana walked alongside Mrs. Thompson as
they all trekked through the airport to the
car outside. "What did Faith tell you, so that

you had no trouble identifying us? That I'm skinny and gangly?"

Shelley interrupted, "And I'm fat and juvenile-looking?"

As they piled into the car Sarah answered for her mother. "Not at all. She wrote that you, Dana, were slim, sophisticated, and chic. And you, Shelley, were cuddly and cute."

Shelley closed her eyes for a moment. "I don't think I've ever heard of a cuddly actress."

As they drove to the Thompson apartment, Sarah and Richie showed them all the points of interest. Shelley and Dana kept turning their heads to catch everything. Dana had been to Washington once when she was ten, and Shelley, of course, had never been there.

The Thompsons lived in a four-story house with a wide front stoop. Other tenants in the house were sitting out on the stoop enjoying the sunny day, and everyone had to be introduced to everyone else. Finally, the Thompsons and Shelley and Dana climbed one flight of stairs to the second floor, where the Thompson's apartment was. It ran through the entire floor and a fresh breeze drifted through its six rooms. Faith dumped her bags in the room that she had always shared with Sarah and took Dana and Shelley to the room they were going to use. It was filled with pennants, posters of football stars, and tanks of fish — and obviously was Richie's.

Shelley turned to Richie and said apologetically, "Richie, we're putting you out of your room. Where will you sleep?"

Richie shrugged with resignation. "It's okay. I'll sleep on the living-room couch. I *always* sleep on the couch when people come to visit."

Joan Thompson smoothed the spreads on the twin beds in the room. "Why don't you two unpack and then I'll fix us some lunch. It will give me a chance to catch up a little with Faithie. I'm not used to having my girl away."

Faith winced slightly. "Ma, please, not 'Faithie.' I'm too big for that."

Mrs. Thompson tapped her on the rear and pushed her out of the room. "You're never too big for me."

Dana and Shelley started to unpack in silence. They both felt the strain of being alone together, and neither knew what to say. Once they would have been laughing and talking excitedly about being there, about plans for the weekend, but now they just moved from their suitcases to the closet to the bureau, awkwardly avoiding each other.

In the kitchen, Faith quickly filled her mother in on what had been going on. "It's just getting worse, Ma. Dana is impatient and really almost mean to Shelley. She doesn't spend much time with us anymore. She is with this Nancy most of the time. Whatever Shelley does or says annoys Dana. And Shelley gets more and more irritating as

Dana gets nastier. And Shelley's feelings are so hurt."

Mrs. Thompson stopped buttering the golden pieces of whole-wheat bread and sighed. She handed Faith a piece of bread. "Eat this."

Faith smiled and started chewing on the bread. "Ma, you have to help. That's why I brought them here. So you could talk to them and make things the way they used to be among us. I *miss* it."

Mrs. Thompson put her arm around Faith. "I'm not a miracle worker, Faithie. Just a social worker. I'll try, but don't expect too much. They really have to work things out for themselves."

In the small dining room, everyone made sandwiches and talked at once, getting to know each other and beginning to sense that the strangeness they felt was fading away little by little.

"Okay," Sarah said. "What do you want to see most?"

"The White House," Dana said.

"The Lincoln Memorial," Shelley said at the same time.

The two girls looked at each other and laughed shyly. "Well," Shelley said, "either one."

They got back into the car and went to the center of Washington. First, Mrs. Thompson just drove around and let the girls see as much as possible from the car. Then, they stopped at some of the monuments. The whole weekend was like that, crammed with sight-seeing and tramping up endless steps and going through room after historical room. Each afternoon they went back to the Thompson apartment exhausted.

Saturday, before dinner, Shelley stretched out on her bed and fell asleep, and Dana went into the kitchen to help Joan Thompson. When she arrived in the kitchen, Faith gave her mother a pleading look and said, "As long as you're providing the kitchen help, Dana, I'm going to make a few phone calls."

As Dana began to peel potatoes, she glanced at Mrs. Thompson out of the corner of her eye. At the same moment, Joan Thompson looked at her.

Dana smiled feebly. "Faith told you, didn't she? About Shelley and me?"

Mrs. Thompson nodded yes.

"I knew that was why Faith wanted us to come here. So you could straighten us out — in a way. But I don't know if it can be done." The words were a little choked in Dana's throat.

Mrs. Thompson walked away from the counter where she was salting chicken pieces and sat down at the kitchen table with Dana. "Do you still like Shelley?" she asked.

Dana looked at Mrs. Thompson, took a deep breath, and answered, "I like the Shelley that was. The one that wasn't the great actress so wound up in her own problems.

Sort of dumb sometimes. But this Shelley —
well, she just makes me mad. And I can't seem
to hide my feelings. I'm the one who has to
make some big decisions, and Shelley acts as
if *she's* the one with the problems."

Mrs. Thompson nodded. "I know. Faith
told me about your father's getting married
and moving to Hawaii. You're right that
you've got a whopping decision to make. But
Shelley probably thinks her problems are just
as whopping. People are like that, you know.
All people think *their* lives and *their* problems are the most important ones."

Dana reached over and took Mrs. Thompson's hand. "What should I do? I want us to
be friends again. I do."

"That's a big question: 'What should I
do?' How about just trying the old count-to-
ten bit? When you're annoyed with her, instead of jumping on her right away, take a
breath, count to ten, and remind yourself
that this is the same Shelley you loved, just
going through a thing."

"You think it'll work?" asked Dana.

"Maybe. But at the same time you have to
remember that you're going through your
own thing, that you're tense and upset, *and*
you have a right to be."

Dana smiled. "I'll try, really I will."

She went back into the bedroom, sat down
on her bed, and watched Shelley sleep. Shelley looked like a kid, with her blond hair
tangled and falling on her face. Her cheeks

were rosy and her mouth was slightly open. Almost as if she felt Dana looking at her, she opened her eyes.

"Hi," Dana said softly.

"Hi," Shelley answered and reached out her hand.

Dana hesitated and then took Shelley's hand for a moment. "Dinner in an hour."

After dinner, Shelley stayed in the kitchen to help Mrs. Thompson clean up, and the rest of the family and Dana went downstairs to sit on the stoop.

"Are you enjoying school, Shelley?" Mrs. Thompson asked.

"It's awfully exciting right now. You see, I'm in this drama club and I've decided I want to be an actress and that means that I have to tell Paul about that and maybe about Tom and —"

Shelley stopped suddenly. "I do that all the time now. I just rattle on and on. I know it."

She put down the dish towel she was holding, sat at the table, and put her head in her hands. "They think I'm dumb, that I don't know why Faith brought us here — to see you — but I'm not dumb. I do know, and I know Dana hates me and sometimes I don't blame her, but I just can't seem to stop being so gabby and . . ."

She started to cry softly, the way she did in any crisis. "I want us to be friends again. I want Dana to stop being so mean to me."

Joan Thompson looked at the bent, blond

head and listened to the muffled sniffing. "You have to remember that Dana is going through a very stressful time, Shelley, that she's confused and unhappy and doesn't have much patience or time to care about other people's problems — even yours. She's scared, Shelley."

Shelley huffed. "Dana is *never* scared."

"Well, she is now!" said Mrs. Thompson.

That night as they got ready for bed, Shelley asked, "Are you scared, Dana?"

Dana turned to her in surprise. Her face paled slightly before she answered, "Yes." That was all, just yes.

Shelley hesitated, then said, "I'm sorry. Can I help?"

Dana shook her head no, but the two girls looked at each other warmly for the first time in a long time.

Sunday was a wonderful day. They all went sight-seeing some more, ate lunch out, and went on a tour of the White House. Shelley and Dana acted the way they used to with each other. They laughed and joked and exchanged ice cream cones and leaned on each other as they climbed more stairs to the tops of more monuments. The girls of Room 407 were happy again.

A gala carload of people took off Sunday afternoon to get the three Canby Hall girls into an airplane back to Massachusetts. The girls were scrunched in the backseat; Mrs. Thompson and Richie were in the front seat.

Sarah had made her farewells at the house, since she had studying to do. They allowed an extra hour to drive around Washington to look at the sights they had missed.

On the plane, the girls had three seats together. They joked about the airline supper, comparing it pretty much to Canby Hall dining hall meals. There were three courses in the airline meal: salad, your choice of meat or chicken with vegetables, and dessert. They mixed and matched. Shelley had three desserts. Faith had one chicken and one meat, and Dana had two salads and one mashed potatoes. Shelley had one mashed potatoes, two carrots. Dana had two rolls; Shelley had one roll. By the time trays were collected, the girls from Canby Hall were dissolved in giggles.

"Hold it, just like that," said Faith as she climbed out of her seat into the aisle, stooped, and got a photograph of her roommates laughing together, friends again.

CHAPTER
ELEVEN

But the weekend didn't have lasting results. Once the girls were back at Canby Hall, it was as though they had never left. They signed in about seven, and immediately after, Dana said, "Hey, I've just got time to see Nancy and tell her about Washington," and left. Then Shelley found three phone messages from Tom, which made her go into the performance.

A few days later, Shelley sat in her French class desperately finishing the previous day's homework in order to hand it in on time. She wasn't sure it was right, but she managed to hand in the paper at the same time everyone else did.

"I solemnly resolve," she said to herself, "I absolutely solemnly resolve that this afternoon I am going to do nothing but study French." There was no rehearsal that day. She had nothing planned to take her away from this resolution. Dana and Faith, especially Faith, had been telling her something she knew: She had better start studying more or she would be in real trouble at school. Shelley realized that in the past few weeks — well, to be honest, it was more than just a few weeks, ever since the play and meeting Tom — she hadn't been paying much attention to her schoolwork. All her grades had slipped, but none quite so obviously as French.

"Yes," she said to herself again as it was time to gather up her books and go outside. "This is my afternoon to concentrate on French homework."

She was making her way resolutely to the dorm to study, when Tom came zooming in through the Canby Hall gates and around past Main Building with a magnificent roar. He was riding a long, sleek, bright blue motorcycle. On his head was a big white helmet, and tied behind him on the passenger seat was another white helmet, waiting.

"Tom!" Shelley exclaimed when he stopped with a flourish next to her. "You really did get it; you really did get a motorcycle —"

"Yep," he said. "Isn't it a beauty?"

Shelley was, after all, a girl who had two brothers. She looked the machine up and down, back and forth, stepped back, smiled, and finally nodded. "It certainly is," she said.

With another flourish, Tom unhooked the passenger helmet and offered it to her.

"A short spin, madam?" he asked.

"Oh, Tom, I *can't*," Shelley said. "I'm getting into serious trouble with French."

Tom's face seemed to collapse with disappointment. He wiped an invisible spot off the chrome handlebar with the sleeve of his jacket. Suddenly, seeing the gesture, Shelley felt she was being ridiculous. What in the world difference would a half-hour or an hour make? Anyway, didn't Tom come all this way from town to show her his motorcycle and take her for a ride? To refuse him would be just plain rude, she was sure. The main thing was that Shelley was melting by just being with Tom, even if she looked as though she was only standing there chatting with him. She was flattered that Tom chose her from among all the girls in the cast of the spring play, and she didn't want to do anything to turn him off. Finally, Shelley had never ridden on a motorcycle, and she wanted to.

That took care of her resolution about French. During Study Hours she would try to memorize some of the idioms she never could remember. But she was behind on an English composition so she had to write that, plus finish the lab report that had been due a week before — and try not to think about Tom.

The following Monday, Shelley squeaked through a French exam with a *D* minus.

"I am going to ask you to go for special study in the afternoons," said Mr. Bernard.

Shelley couldn't believe it. "Oh, no," she exclaimed.

That meant an hour and a half or two hours every afternoon with the other girls who were failing, or on the edge of failing, a subject. It was humiliating, but more than that it might get in the way of the most important thing in her life!

"But I'm in the spring play, Mr. Bernard," Shelley protested.

"Well, I'm sure you can arrange your special study schedule so it won't interfere with rehearsals. But remember, Shelley, rehearsals also must not interfere with your academic work. I don't like to see you slipping so badly. I must say that your oral work, your work on the tapes in Language Lab, is not bad. Your accent is quite respectable . . ."

"That's probably because I intend to be an actress. Actresses have to be able to imitate sounds, things like that," Shelley interrupted.

"I see," said Mr. Bernard. "Still, the oral work is the *only* reason you are not actually failing French right now."

The thought of her theatrical voice, which had intrigued Shelley for an instant, blanked out. In its place came the recognition that what Mr. Bernard was saying was serious. Shelley began to feel very frightened. She was acutely aware that finals were looming; finals determined your mark for practically the whole term.

She walked slowly into the dorm, hoping

to avoid meeting Alison, but it just so happened — or could Alison have been waiting? — that they did meet.

"Well, Shelley," Alison said. "They just notified me that you're to have special study every afternoon from now on."

Shelley felt double vibrations come from Alison: a severity that showed Alison's disapproval of Shelley's slack performance in French, and a warmth that meant sympathy and support. It was part of Alison's magic that she could project both feelings at one time. It left Shelley with a sense not that she was the worst girl in the whole school, but that she was surely going to apply herself more than she had been doing to fulfill her own and Alison's expectations.

Nobody was in Room 407 when Shelley got there. The sign-out sheet on the door told her that Dana would not be at school for dinner; she and Nancy and another girl from Addison House, Jennifer Johnson, had gone to the pizza place in town. Faith had not signed out, Shelley noticed with relief.

Once in the room, Shelley turned to face the long mirror on the back of the door.

Just look at you, she said to herself.

She felt cold, thinking her thoughts. If she failed French, she'd have to repeat the whole course. She'd hate that. And how would she explain it to her mother? How would she tell her father? Her brothers wouldn't think very much of her; nobody in their family ever failed in school. What would Paul think? Maybe he would think, *Well, that's not a girl I want to be associated with anyway.* Tom might think it was cute, a funny thing. He thought lots of things were funny things. He might just think the disappointment would help her become a greater actress. *That's exactly what he would think,* Shelley decided.

She put her face closer to the mirror and earnestly searched her forehead for an *L* there. When she was a little girl and given to telling stories that were not always true, her mother used to say, "I see a little white *L* on your forehead." The *L* stood for lie. Shelley knew she was telling herself a lie right now. Tom would never think it was cute if she failed a subject. Nobody would think it was cute, including herself.

She reached for a can of Tab that was on the bookcase near the door. As she reached, she kept her eyes on the reflection of herself in the mirror. She thought she was moving in a graceful way. In one scene in the play, she had to pick up a book from a table. She put the Tab down, picked it up again, studying the look of herself in the mirror.

"That's the gesture I'll use," she said out loud.

Holding the unopened Tab, Shelley stood in front of the mirror again and observed herself. She decided she looked like a tragic character. Her face was paler than usual, she thought. She was still plump, but recently, because of Thespians, because of Jane Fonda's exercises, there was a new, lithe, straighter look to her.

She willed herself to slump into a sad pose. The can slipped out of her hand, but Shelley hardly noticed. She was very absorbed in seeing herself, the great actress, bowing to the audience as it applauded her performance.

Faith pushed the door open just as Shelley was reaching out to receive a final bouquet of flowers from the imaginary audience.

"Hey, kid, are you all right?" Faith asked.

"Sure," said Shelley.

"I saw you tooling around on that shiny blue bike of Tom's," Faith said.

"Yeah!" said Shelley, grinning, no longer the tragic actress in any way. "It was great. You know, when you go around a corner on a motorcycle, it kind of leans over and you do, too."

But while she watched Faith drop books, handbag, and jacket in the middle of the floor — and wrap the strap of her camera around the case and carefully put the camera in its own place in the top drawer of her bureau — Shelley remembered her new trouble and wondered if she wanted to tell Faith about it. She decided she wasn't going to say anything. She wouldn't tell anybody. It wasn't so important. She was pretty sure that all she needed was one concentrated week of afternoon special study and French would be okay. She wasn't even going to *think* about it.

What she *did* think was that she would definitely apply to Carnegie-Mellon's Drama Department when she was a senior. She might even send for the catalogues now, so she would be all prepared when the time came.

Faith's clothes began to join her other things in a pile in the middle of the floor. Wrapping herself in her big terry-cloth robe that had been lying on her bed since morning, Faith grabbed her shower cap and vanished down the hall in the direction of the bathroom. Alone again, Shelley suddenly felt scared inside, and tears that she couldn't control were streaming down her face.

CHAPTER TWELVE

A few days later, Faith slogged back from the *Clarion*. It was getting tiresome, really tiresome, watching Dana take off in the afternoons, and sometimes evenings, with Bret, and then hearing Shelley moaning over two — count 'em — two men in her life, poor dear Paul at home and Tom Terrific, who was around all the time these days.

"All the more reason for you to say yes to Ray Dixon," said Grace. The girls had just finished their latest collaborative piece for the *Clarion* — photographs by Faith Thompson, captions by Grace Barish — and were talking about accepting the invitations that had come from Oakley Prep for the opening of the school's photography show the following Saturday.

"But I don't get it," Grace persisted. "Why shouldn't he be great?"

"Because," said Faith. She was already re-

gretting having confided her case of the
downs to Grace.

"Because he's Oakley? And their paper's
photographer? I must be pretty dumb, but I
think the fact that you're both photographers
on your school papers gives you something in
common," Grace said.

"Sure it does," Faith agreed. She paused
for a moment. Could she share with Grace
the rest of the odd set of feelings she seemed
to be having? Only part of it was the fact that
both her roommates were involved with boy-
friends and she wasn't. Another part, the
part that concerned Raymond Dixon, seemed
to come from someplace else.

"I think I'm just having a case of the
blahs." That was all she could tell Grace.
Suddenly, for no reason in the world, Faith
found herself comparing Raymond Dixon to
her father but not wanting to say so.

Grace waited but no more was forthcom-
ing.

"You know what?" Grace said. "No matter
what's going on in your head right now,
you'll hate yourself in the morning if you
don't go to that show with Ray."

"Okay. I'll go," Faith said.

"I can't get over your enthusiasm."

In fact, Faith was anxious the whole time
she was getting ready for her date with Raymond, which delighted Shelley and Dana.
They had always valued Faith for her

strengths — her common sense, good humor, balance, and her wit. Now they were happily sharing a switch: Dana and Shelley were a team, being strong and supportive, while Faith struggled with the nervousness she felt before her first real date at school. It would be a brief unity between Shelley and Dana. Shelley had a date with Tom to see a classic old movie that was in town, and Dana was meeting Bret at the photo exhibit later. The plan was for Dana and Bret and Faith and Ray to go out for a pizza afterward.

"You're not going to back out, are you?" Faith asked Dana with an expression on her face that was part pout and part panic.

"Of course not," Dana said.

"Because I don't mind being with Raymond Dixon looking at pictures, but I don't want a whole evening with him."

"I don't understand you, Faith. Ray's a nice guy," Dana said.

Faith sighed. *You're nuts*, she said to herself later, as she was going down the stairs to the lounge where Ray was waiting.

What Dana said about him is true, she thought as Ray came toward her, smiling, saying hi. He certainly was good-looking, tall, thin with wide-set eyes, high cheek bones, and skin the color of burnished copper. His hair was cut in a close natural; Faith found herself figuring she was in the presence of a forty-dollar styling job.

"Hey, Faith, I'm glad to see you."

"Hi, Ray."

He was dressed perfectly enough to almost make her shake her head: good jeans, blue blazer, oxford cloth shirt. It was *too* preppy. Faith didn't think her roommates, or Grace, or any of her white friends at Canby Hall would understand if she told them how she, daughter of a cop and a social worker from inner-city D.C., was put off by Ray's style. She simply didn't like his super-easy "Good-evening" to Alison, the way he bent to reach around Faith to open the door to go out, his new, sleek little car waiting outside.

Once at Oakley, though, in the student lounge that had been turned into a photography gallery, she was glad she had come. The pictures were very good.

"This is sensational," she said to Ray as they approached a huge color print of a stone wall — a school wall patterned with ivy — a pale yet striking photograph. "It really has it all," she added, studying the picture carefully. "I'm impressed."

"Thanks," Ray said.

"Is it yours? she asked, surprised. *Maybe the date won't be a total loss*, she thought.

After a few hours at the exhibit, everyone seemed to have the same idea: pizza. The pizza place, Pizza Pete, was jammed when Dana and Faith, Bret and Ray, and some of their friends — Grace, a pal of Bret's named

Mark Goldsmith, Molly Jonas from Canby Hall — arrived and managed to fit themselves into a corner booth. Everybody was talking about everything, Faith and Ray comparing notes on camera angles, lenses, lighting, and some of the photographs they had all just seen.

For Dana, chatting away with the others, it was fun to see Faith and Ray seeming to like each other. She looked at them and put her hand out under the table, reaching for Bret's hand. There was a responsive, comforting squeeze from him, although he didn't turn toward her. He seemed to be listening to the story Ray was telling and looking to make sure Faith was enjoying Ray's story, too.

The crowding was fun, the pizza was fun. They had ordered the kind with everything on it, and even the waiter who brought it over admired it. There was only one troubling note.

"That's rough about Shelley," Molly said to Dana.

"What about Shelley?"

"She's flunking French and has to go to special study."

"I don't believe it!" Dana said.

"It's true. I'm in her French class. I know it's true. Didn't she tell you?"

Dana glanced toward Faith, but she seemed too involved for Dana to interrupt.

Suddenly, it was close to curfew. As they walked toward Oakley Hall, the boys' school,

Bret picked a forsythia sprig from a bush they passed and gave it to Dana. She twirled it between her fingers. The Massachusetts air had its own special crispness, a no-nonsense quality that announced springtime in a peculiarly invigorating New England style.

"It's going to be summer vacation before you turn around," Bret observed.

"Don't say that," Dana exclaimed.

"Okay," said Bret.

They walked in silence. They had pulled back behind the others to walk together up the hill.

Despite herself, Dana laughed. "You can say it if you want to," she said.

"Once is enough," Bret said. "But I was leading up to something."

"Lead on," Dana said.

He immediately put his arm around her and they started dancing cheek-to-cheek, humming.

"I'm leading," he said as he twirled her up the sidewalk in a fairly good imitation of '40s dancing. They both laughed.

"Do you know what you're going to do about Hawaii yet, Dana?" Bret asked seriously as they broke apart.

"No, I don't," Dana said.

"I'm really . . . I wish I could help you, Dana. I hate to see you unhappy about anything." He put his arms around her and kissed her gently. She hugged him hard and thought, *How can I leave Bret?*

CHAPTER THIRTEEN

By the time they decided to use Ray's car — "because it's prettier than Bret's," as Ray put it with a smooth grin — and were on their way, the girls realized they had exactly four and a half minutes to be in their dorm. It worried them all the way home and cut the good-byes down to a few quick waves of hands.

Once they were inside Baker House, though, they breathed a sigh of relief. They were late, but not so late that it mattered.

"No Shelley," Dana announced when she opened the door to their room. She glanced at her watch. It was now almost fifteen minutes after curfew. "We're late enough, but at least we're here. That idiot girl is going to get herself into even more trouble if she doesn't show up pretty fast."

Dana could see Faith tense up.

"Come on, Faith. Cut it out. That wasn't a nasty remark. Tonight I heard that Shelley's in trouble in French. I mean she's really flunking."

"That's bad," Faith said. "Remember, we used to have our French salon and study together? She's avoided it for months now."

"Our roommate's been goofing around so much that now she's got to go to afternoon special study."

Faith whistled. "She didn't say a word about it to me. But . . ." She paused. "Now that I think back, she looked a little teary the other day."

"I'm honestly sorry," Dana said sincerely. "And before you say anything, I'm for doing everything we can to help. I mean, I'll stand over her with a French dictionary ready to bop her whenever she needs it."

They could hear feet running frantically down the hall and then their door burst open. Shelley, sparkling-eyed, blond hair tossed over her flushed cheeks, exploded into the room.

"Quick, before Alison comes and puts me in jail because I'm so late, tell me every single thing about your date, Faith."

She was almost irresistible, but Dana managed to resist. Dana went over to the window and gazed out, her back to the room. Then she came back and, as though the others weren't even there, walked toward her bureau pulling her sweater over her head as she went. She carefully folded it and put it away in her drawer. She continued walking around the room, getting ready for bed as Faith and Shelley, curled on Faith's bed, watched her. Finally both of them shrugged and turned toward each other.

"Okay, Faith, tell all," Shelley said.

"There isn't so much to tell. We did just what we were going to do — looked at pictures, right?"

"Come on!" Shelley exclaimed.

"And then, just as planned, we went out for pizza . . ." she went on, straight-faced.

"Faith, don't *do* that," Shelley interrupted with a grin. "Did you like being with him? Are you going to see him again? Let's hear the important things!"

"Okay," said Faith, shrugging. "First thing, sure I liked being with him. He's a very nice guy — maybe a little preppy, which isn't my style, but he's okay."

"Good," Shelley said.

Dana, a little embarrassed at the way she had been pointedly ignoring them, pushed her silky brown hair back from her eyes, flopped down on the bed, and joined in.

"Truth is, isn't it, Faith, that he's really cute . . . and bright . . . and talented?" Dana said.

"Sure, and —" Faith got up abruptly and went over to the pyramid of Tabs and took a can. "Anyone else want one?" she asked. When they both shook their heads, she came back and resettled herself on the bed. "What can I say? I'm sort of just not all that impressed."

Shelley made a mournful sound. "I wanted you to fall madly in love with him."

Dana considered Faith's answer seriously. "What do you really want in a guy?" she asked.

"Someone like my father," Faith answered. "Only *not* a cop."

Okay. That's that, Shelley thought and rolled over and onto the floor. Faith and Dana exchanged glances. Dana shrugged. Faith nodded.

"Shelley," Faith began, "sit down on that chair and start to listen to something more important than my feelings about Raymond Dixon."

Shelley, surprised, sat down.

"What's this about you and French? Wait! Don't even answer. We know."

"What do you know?" Shelley demanded.

"Oh, come off it, Shelley," Dana said sharply.

"We know you're at the bottom in French," Faith hurriedly continued. "What's more, we also know we're not going to let you mess up your schoolwork, even if you do want to be the world's greatest actress."

"You don't have to worry about me, Faith. I'm going to work very hard. I solemnly promised myself."

"Good," Faith said, "but we're going to make sure you stick to that promise."

Shelley glanced at Dana.

"Yes, me, too, Shel. I'm in on this as much as Faith is."

Shelley smiled weakly. "Except what are you in on? I'm the one who has to do it."

"Obviously," Dana said.

"How badly are you doing, Shelley?" Faith asked flatly.

"Well, my work in Language Lab is pretty good, Mr. Bernard said."

"That doesn't take in vocabulary, idioms, grammar — past subjunctives, for instance." Dana said.

Shelley made a face. "I just find those things very *hard*."

"We better find out how much you know," Dana said. "Where's your textbook?"

Dana, the language buff, took Shelley's French book in hand and leafed through it.

"Okay," she said, "I'll start with the very first lesson. "Conjugate *avoir*." Dana looked at her round-faced roommate's eyes. There was the start of a suggestion of tears. "Shelley, just conjugate the verb *avoir*. Don't cry." Dana spoke as calmly as she could.

After Shelley painfully got through the conjugation, Dana went here and there through the book, touching on the things she'd mentioned — idioms, vocabulary, grammar, and translation, including the following

Monday's translation assignment. Shelley stumbled over it as though she had never read a syllable in French before.

"Disaster," Dana announced finally. "Shelley, where has your head been?" She found that she felt too sorry for Shelley to be annoyed with her. "When're your finals?"

"I'm not absolutely sure," Shelley said. "In three weeks, I think. I'll find out tomorrow. I'll be at Main Building, and I'll find out."

"Tomorrow's Sunday, Shelley," said Dana, the now familiar note of exasperation entering her voice.

"Well, I'm meeting Tom and some of the other kids from the spring play at Main tomorrow," Shelley said. "One of them's in French with me. She'll know."

"Have you thought about staying here and maybe working on some of that translation instead?" Faith said quickly, before Dana had a chance to say anything.

"Tomorrow night, I promise," Shelley said earnestly. "But I have to meet them. We're going to read some scenes from Shakespeare, to develop our vowel sounds, Tom says."

"Shelley!" Dana exclaimed. "I can't believe you."

Faith simply threw herself on her bed and covered her head with the pillow.

"I think it really could be bad news, even with her taking special study," Dana said as she and Faith talked it over the next afternoon, after Shelley had left for her reading. "She isn't with it at all."

"I feel kind of responsible," Faith said. "And I hope you feel the same way. We used to have a pretty good buddy system operating in Room 407. If we still had it, you and I would have known about this before it got serious."

"You're right," Dana agreed, feeling waves of guilt. "That's why I want you to know that what I said last night still goes. I'm for doing whatever we can to help. I mean, we can't let Shelley flunk a course." She meant what she was saying but suddenly had a thought: *If I lived in Hawaii, I wouldn't have to worry about this.* Quickly she brushed the thought away and tried to make a little joke. "Can't let down the honor of 407."

"How do you think we should work it?" Faith asked, feeling relief at Dana's attitude.

"I don't know. What do you think?"

They both sat silently for a moment.

"There's only one way," Faith said finally. "We're going to have to set aside some time and tutor her."

Dana sighed. "I knew you were going to say that."

"I'm right, aren't I?"

Dana sighed again. "Yes, you are. It'll mean juggling our schedules around. When do we all ever have the same free time?"

"The answer to that is never," Faith said. "Let's try to figure it out. I think I know Shel's rehearsal schedule . . ."

"Who doesn't?" Dana said, feeling angry once again.

"And you've got — what, the choir on Wednesdays and Latin Club . . ."

"And Bret, don't forget. And don't forget you. *Clarion* almost every day and going out on stories when you're not in the office. Oh, Faith, you don't have a minute."

"We'll just have to squeeze it in. After Study Hours?"

"No," said Dana emphatically.

They bounced the possibilities back and forth, until they finally came up with the hour before dinner on two different days for tutoring Shelley. Dana would cut out her jogging on Thursday to accommodate an hour Faith was free. Faith in her turn would give up one of her favorite activities, roaming the campus with her camera to shoot nature shots, so she could be available during Dana's open hour on Tuesdays. It fit Shelley's schedule and was workable but meant both girls would be giving up some of their precious free time.

"And we'll have to pray a lot," Dana said, thinking of the mess Shelley had made of a list of important idioms.

After they had it settled, Faith and Dana separated for the afternoon. Dana went to a movie with Nancy, and Faith wandered in the orchard for a while practicing close-up photography on buds and leaves. After that, putting off going back to the dorm, Faith met a couple of her *Clarion* co-workers and went with them to the Tutti-Frutti for some ice cream.

"How was the big date?" asked Grace. "Yesterday. With Ray?"

"I forget," Faith answered, attacking her sundae.

CHAPTER FOURTEEN

*D*ear Dad,

I know it's been a long time since you heard from me, but that doesn't mean I haven't been thinking about you. How do you like Honolulu? You wouldn't believe how much time I've spent looking up the Hawaiian Islands in the encyclopedia in the library. Crazy names! I mean, how does anybody pronounce Kohala or Niihau?

I guess you're wondering whether I'm coming to Honolulu. I have to tell you, Dad, I've been so busy here at school that I haven't had time to make up my mind. I hope it's okay with you if I let you know later on. Do I have a deadline??!

Dana put her pen down and sat back in the bean-bag chair, her favorite chair in Nancy's room. Nancy was across the room at her desk, totally absorbed, bending over her sketch pad. There were little pots of water-

122

colors on the desk, as well as a cup of water and another cup holding brushes. Dana had begun to find Nancy's room more pleasant and comfortable than her own when she had a little time free — like now. Soon she would have to be going back to Baker House for the tutoring session with Shelley.

She didn't know what to write next. She wasn't sure her father would be all that interested in the goings-on at Canby Hall, especially if she decided to go and live with him. Canby Hall would then be just x-ed out of her life for an entire year.

Go to live with him and Eve, she thought. Dana knew she had to stop thinking about her father as someone without Eve. She had to think about her father from now on, and always, as Dad and Eve. June wasn't far away — June, when they were going to be married, and she would be going to the wedding. *Mom!* she cried in her thoughts.

Suddenly, the letter she was writing upset her, and she hurried to finish it.

Well, Dad, I have to go now. Take care.
Love and kisses, Dana.

She stirred in the chair and Nancy looked up briefly. "How's it going?" she murmured, still absorbed in her drawing.

"Oh, a letter to my father," Dana said.

"Telling him yes or no?"

Dana shook her head. "Telling him I still don't know," she said. She picked up her pen again.

P.S. she wrote, and paused. She always felt she had to mention Eve in a letter to her father and had the same problem every time she wrote. She didn't really want to add, "When you write to her, say love to Eve." She wished there were some perfect phrase to use instead. She had tried out several: "When you talk to Eve, send my hello." "Regards to Eve." "Season's greetings to Eve!!!!" Dana sighed and decided on the same thing she always ended up with: *Hi to Eve,* she wrote. She added an exclamation mark, studied the effect, then pulled the letter out of her loose-leaf notebook, and started to fold it. Nancy pushed her sketch pad away, stood up, and stretched. She looked down at the painting she had been working on and then gave her full attention to Dana.

"Need an envelope?" she asked.

"If you have one."

Nancy rummaged in a desk drawer and triumphantly held up a white envelope.

"Interested in a stamp?" she asked, and rummaging again, produced one.

"Fantastic," Dana said, laughing. She put the letter in the envelope, addressed and stamped it, sealed it, and over the back flap wrote "SWAK."

Head cocked to one side, Nancy picked up her painting and studied it.

"Finished?" Dana asked.

"I think so," Nancy said.

She held the sketch pad out for Dana to see.

"Why, it's me," Dana said in surprise. "I didn't know you were drawing me."

Nancy grinned. "I know. You were really far away."

"It's good, Nancy, if I can say that about a painting of myself," Dana said, impressed as always by Nancy's talent.

"You can say it as much as you want to." Nancy laughed.

Dana looked more carefully at the painting. With quick strokes of watercolor, Nancy had caught her concentrating completely, hunched over her letter, hair falling on her shoulder. Dana looked more closely at the face in the drawing.

"Nancy, do I really look . . . so sad?" she asked softly.

"You've been having a hard time lately," Nancy said sympathetically. "Maybe it shows."

"Okay. Run through it again. 'If I were going to the . . .' — that last bit of translation," Faith said, the book in her hand.

"Oh, not again," Shelley wailed. The girls in 407 were into their tutoring session.

"Go on. Do it," Dana said sharply. "Again till you get it."

Dana couldn't sit still. She was pacing up

and down, exasperated. Faith had read the start of the translation four times. Each time Shelley had repeated it, gone on to the next sentence, struggled through the sentence after that, and when Faith said, "From the beginning now," forgotten the first phrase.

"I'm terribly sorry, Faith," Shelley said, as though she were apologizing for having to leave a party early.

"It's not all right," Faith heard herself saying, just as politely. Faith then collapsed and Dana took over.

"Look, Shel. Let's just forget the beginning. You have a block or something. Start in the middle of the page."

"Can't we do something else?" Shelley pleaded. "I'll do this alone, I promise. I'll do it in my special study."

"I could give up on it," Faith said, shaking her head, "except that we shouldn't."

"How about we switch over to idioms for a while. What do you think?" Dana asked Faith.

"It's up to you," Faith said. "You're the French expert. I'm just the desperate disciplinarian."

"What about me? You can ask me, too," Shelley said indignantly.

"Shelley, honestly, I don't think you understand how terribly ignorant you are in all this."

"Please don't say things like that, Dana." Shelley was close to tears. "I'm trying, but it

doesn't do any good. I don't *want* to fail."
Now the tears were starting to flow.

"Shelley, don't you *dare* cry. We have work
to do. Now, come on, I'll read you some
phrases in English, and you tell me the
French idiom." Dana glared at her.

Shelley sniffled a little. Then she shook her
head. "Oh, I don't know why I have to do this.
After all, when I become an actress and have
to say something in French, someone else
will tell me what the words mean. I'll only
have to be able to pronounce them right."

"Uh-huh," Dana said, her lips tightening.

"Even Mr. Bernard says my accent's very
good." Shelley went on, not noticing the
growing, almost ominous, feeling in the
room. "I'm still going to be an actress even if
it's very hard on many people — on Paul,
for instance — but that's still my ambition.
That's my goal."

"Well, my goal," Dana said, interrupting,
"is to help you through this French. So come
on. I'm here. Faith's here. You're here. Let's
get this done. I'll read you some English, and
you tell me the French idioms. What's the
idiom for 'See you later'?"

Shelley immediately looked abashed.
"You're right, Dana. You're both being really
wonderful. I'm honestly sorry if I'm giving
you a hard time."

"That's better," Dana said. "Let's go
now . . ."

* * *

It had been ten days since they had started their tutoring program, and after every session Dana had to admit she felt angry inside.

"I'm glad I'm doing it, honestly I am, Nancy," Dana said to her friend later, when they met on the cafeteria line in the dining hall. Dana now chose to have dinner with Nancy rather than with Faith and Shelley. "It's just the thing that gets me is that Shelley takes it all so casually. She still gives the performance all the time, and I don't think she should — it's that simple. Can you imagine how she'd act if she really had a problem? *Mine*, for instance?"

"Well, I think you're being great," said Nancy as they carried their trays to a table near the enormous picture window that looked over some of Canby Hall's prettiest lawns, trees, and gardens.

"Thanks," Dana said.

"Talking about your problem, how about Hawaii?" Nancy asked.

"Don't I wish I knew," Dana answered.

CHAPTER FIFTEEN

The following week, Dana found out that choir rehearsal had been switched from Wednesday to Thursday because one of the singers, Sarah Lund, who also played the cello, was having an audition in Boston for a statewide high school summer orchestra.

Dana had a struggle with herself: Should she skip the tutoring session with Shelley or should she skip the rehearsal? They were at the same time.

Dana wanted to go to choir. She really enjoyed singing and always looked forward to the weekly practice. She also wanted to hang around with the other choristers and hear about Sarah's audition. On the other hand, she knew she had an obligation to Faith as well as Shelley. Helping Shelley was a joint Room 407 undertaking that she could not back out of. All this was going through her head as she came out of Main Building with Jackie Adams, who was on her way to choir.

"Dana, do you know what you're doing?" Jackie said.

"No, what?"

"You're muttering."

Dana laughed. "I bet I am," she said. Then a small frown appeared between her brows. It was the one that was on her forehead often these days, the one Nancy had caught in her watercolor portrait. It appeared whenever Dana had to make a decision, but choir versus tutoring was a fairly cut-and-dried question, and the frown soon vanished.

"Listen, Jackie," she said. "I'm not going to rehearsal today. If Mr. Brewster says anything, will you please just tell him I have something crucial to do?"

"Sure. No problem."

"Thanks," said Dana.

"Nothing." Then, as the girls started to walk across the campus, "I sure wish Sarah good luck," Jackie added.

"Me, too," Dana said. "I didn't even know she was trying for it. It'll be sensational if she makes it."

"Much honor to the lioness," Jackie said.

Dana laughed. Then she looked at her watch. "Oops. Gotta go," she said, not wanting to.

Faith showed up in Room 407 a moment after Dana.

"I think I'm learning as much French as

Shelley is," she said, picking up Shelley's French workbook.

"I thought we might work on some vocabulary stuff today," Dana said. "I made up this sensational long list of foods. That should keep her interested."

Both girls laughed as they waited for Shelley. Faith kicked off her sneakers and picked up the newest issue of *General Photographer*, which had just arrived. Dana went over her list. "I forgot asparagus," she said.

"Add it," Faith mumbled.

There was a pleasant silence as Dana looked over the vocabulary list and Faith got more immersed in her magazine. Soon both girls began to realize the silence was stretching out, that they were waiting longer than they should have for Shelley to arrive.

Dana put the list aside and sighed. "I got a letter from my dad today," she said.

Faith looked up from her magazine. "Is he still out there?"

"Yes, in Honolulu."

Faith settled back into her magazine, and Dana into her thoughts. More time went by. Then Faith finished with the magazine, sat cross-legged on her bed, and looked at Dana.

"You haven't been talking about Hawaii very much lately," she said gently. "Have you made up your mind yet? Do we have our roommate next year or are we going to lose you?"

"I don't know," Dana answered, warmed by the concern in Faith's words. "It's like a big question mark in my head all the time. I can never shake it. It really haunts me."

Suddenly Dana began to feel explosive. She got up and started to pace the room.

"I still just can't decide. When I talk to my mother, I think, how can I possibly go away from her? How can I go away for a whole year and leave her?"

Faith made a comforting, listening sound. She slipped down to the floor, head resting against her bed, long legs stretched out.

"And Maggie," Dana went on in a rush, "you know, my sister to me is like Richie to you. I'd never see my mother and I'd never see Maggie." Dana stopped short and even stopped pacing and said, almost desperately trying for a laugh, "I'm making it sound like exile to Siberia, aren't I?"

"Maybe a little," Faith agreed.

Dana started pacing again.

"And how can I leave you . . . and Bret?" She continued, a little more calmly but with the frown back between her brows, "I get a letter from Dad, and he definitely wants me with him and he definitely loves me a lot. And I love him. And Eve . . . I've read you some of her notes to me, right? Eve is really okay. Sometimes I think it might be great to live with them for a year." The frown deepened between Dana's brows. "Only I don't know. I mean, I just don't *know* yet."

Neither girl spoke for a moment. Then suddenly, abruptly, Dana banged the flat of her hand against the top of her desk.

"Where *is* Shelley?" she demanded. "And I really wanted to go to choir. Darn that girl! We've been waiting for her for almost a whole hour."

"I'm with you," Faith said, "but let's keep it cool. I'm sure there's a good reason."

"I can tell you just what the reason is," Dana said. "As a matter of fact, I can hear it." She went over to the window and looked down. "I was right. I knew I heard Tom's motorcycle. Shelley's riding on it."

"I don't believe it!" Faith said.

"I'm beginning to think we can believe anything about Shelley." Dana turned from the window and faced the door, her eyes blazing.

"Come on now, Dana. Cool off." Faith opened the door, stepped out into the hall, and seeing Shelley just at the top of the stairs, waved to her to hurry into the room.

"I guess I'm late," Shelley said breathlessly as both her roommates faced her accusingly.

"I guess you are." Dana's voice was dangerously quiet.

"I couldn't be sorrier. Rehearsal, you know. And then I was with Tom."

"What a surprise," Dana said in the same tone.

"I told him I had to get back here, but we got so engrossed in our conversation, he forgot and I guess I just didn't notice how late it was getting."

"Poor Shelley." Dana was bitingly sarcastic.

"Oh, no," Shelley protested. "It was awful of me. But you know . . . let's skip this session. I mean, with special study yesterday and that rehearsal this afternoon, well, I just don't feel like doing French now. I feel . . . I feel . . . after the rehearsal and all, I don't want to come back to such things. It's hard to express in words."

"Express it in action, Shelley," Dana said. "The following action: Sit down in that chair, pick up that book, and translate what's on page one forty-four."

"Don't speak to me that way, Dana," Shelley said. "I appreciate what you're doing for me, helping me and all, but I think sometimes you're not very nice about it."

"Nice?!" Dana exploded.

Faith quickly tried to turn off the argument. "Stop it! My time's too important for this kind of stuff. Let's get going."

"I didn't do anything," Shelley said.

"You came in late," Dana answered angrily. "You kept both of us waiting. We've been giving up our precious time for you, and you come breezing in almost an hour late, riding up on that motorcycle. I must say you are a champion thoughtless girl."

"Now, wait a minute," Faith said. "Let's keep things under control here. Are we going to tutor or aren't we?"

The heat was growing in the room. Neither Shelley nor Dana seemed to hear Faith at all. Shelley stamped her foot.

"You're cruel and you're mean and you're not understanding," she shouted at Dana.

"And you're just childish and selfish," Dana shouted back. "You're a baby."

"I'm trying," Shelley cried. "You expect so much of people. You don't have any sympathy for anybody who's not as perfect as you think you are."

"Compared to you, I *am* perfect. You've been a bore. And I don't have time for you anymore."

Faith jumped up and put herself between Dana and Shelley, as though to keep them from even looking at each other.

"Listen, you both have to *stop* this," she exclaimed. "You're saying things you're going to be sorry about. Neither of you means it."

"I mean every word," Dana said.

"So do I." Shelley burst into tears. "I used to think you were wonderful, Dana. Well, I don't anymore. I think you're mean and a snob."

"I can't stand you, Shelley Hyde," Dana exclaimed as she stormed out of the room, her face flushed with fury and unhappiness.

"Well, I don't care, because she *is*," Shelley cried at Faith.

"Leave me out of this," Faith exclaimed, almost in tears herself. "I've had it up to here with both of you. This was a great tutoring session. I'm going to dinner." Then Faith left.

"I'm going to study," Shelley sobbed, crying out after her.

The anger and discord between Shelley and Dana — and Faith, too — was as tangible as smoke. It even affected other girls on the floor. They didn't know what had happened, but that night when Gloria Palmer sneaked into 407 during Study Hours to announce a forbidden midnight pig-out in Casey's room, she knew things were bad. The three girls were at their desks, but the atmosphere was freezing. Shelley had her head in her arms. She looked up for a moment and immediately hid her face again, but not before Gloria saw that it was puffy and her eyes were red from crying. Dana didn't look up at all. She just waved without turning around. Faith was the only one mildly polite, and even Faith's usually unruffled expression was tight.

"Hey," said Gloria softly, but aware of the thunderclouds. "I came to invite you to a party later. Casey got a 'CARE' package and everyone's invited."

Gloria had been doing this up and down the hall. She was having fun doing it, sneaking into rooms and whispering her message, sneaking out and into the next room before Alison discovered her. But there was no fun in Room 407. Gloria delivered her message and waited for a moment.

"Thanks," Faith said.

"I'll try to come," Shelley said, gulping but not raising her head from her hands.

"Sorry. Another time," Dana managed to say.

Gloria made a fast exit. "Something really serious is going on in there," she said to her roommate Jackie when she got back to her own room.

CHAPTER SIXTEEN

The fury of the fight in Room 407 did not dissipate. The room was like an armed camp. Shelley and Dana spoke to each other only when they absolutely had to, and Faith was so upset she finally phoned her mother.

"Look, Faithie," Joan Thompson said. "You've done as much as you can. Now you just have to let it alone. It's up to them, not you." This didn't make Faith feel any better.

For Dana, nothing helped, not even jogging. Three days after the fight, she had been jogging around the playing field almost an hour, but it hadn't done any good. She felt miserable. Everything was awful. She didn't even really *feel* like jogging. She wanted to go to her room and do nothing. But it wasn't easy, the way it used to be, to just hang out in 407. Dana always avoided being in her room if she didn't have to be, in case Shelley was there.

Suddenly she remembered that it was Shelley's afternoon for special study. She knew Faith was at the *Clarion*. *How could I have forgotten Shelley would be away?* she wondered, feeling really disturbed, almost confused. Dana stopped jogging and started to run from the playing field toward Baker House. She felt tears gathering in her eyes.

When she got to her room, the tears burst out and overflowed and once inside, she gave herself up to them completely. They streamed down her face as she threw herself on her bed, clenching her hands into fists against the pillow, sobbing, gulping, her whole body caught in convulsive crying.

After a long while, it all started to subside and she began to catch her breath. She got up, wiped her eyes, blew her nose a couple of times, and sat down to try to figure out where she was at.

The tears didn't come again, but an awful feeling of helplessness did. She felt she just couldn't cope with life at Canby Hall anymore. All the new tensions and miseries at the dorm created too many problems on top of the problems she already had. They were swarming through her head. Shelley made her feel miserable, and it was awful sharing a room with her. Faith had retreated into a disapproval that made her seem far away even when she was within touching distance.

Even outside the dorm, it was hard to cope. She'd be coming from a class and think she saw Shelley in the hall and try to avoid her.

It was really terrible. She hated just walking across the campus or stopping at the Student Center because she always had the feeling that Shelley was around every corner. Trying to get rid of that feeling was —

"Dana Morrison, telephone for you," a voice rang out, interrupting her thoughts.

I want out, Dana thought, blowing her nose. With one last sniff, pushing her hair back behind her ear, she went downstairs. She hoped it was Bret. He would cheer her up. Bret wasn't a problem, at least not at the moment.

"Hi!" she said, absolutely sure it was Bret.

"Hi, yourself, Dana, honey." It was her father.

"Oh . . . oh, hi, Dad," she said weakly.

"Hey, have you got a cold or something? You sound funny." His voice was warm, concerned, loving.

"No, no. I'm okay," she answered. "Where are you calling from?"

"New York. I'm just here for a couple of days, and then I go back to Honolulu again. I'd love to see you. Any chance of your coming home for the weekend?"

"Oh, Dad, I can't. It's Thursday already," Dana answered.

"I know this is very short notice. Next time I'll try to arrange it better," her father said.

"Okay," said Dana.

"How's everything going, Dana? I boast to

everybody that I've got a daughter who speaks Latin like a native."

Dana made a small sound that was almost a laugh. "A native of what?"

There was a pause.

"Are you all right, Dana?" said her father, his concern for her traveling over the telephone wire.

"Sure, Dad. Dad . . . I'm going to live with you and Eve in Hawaii."

"What?!"

Dana could hardly believe herself. She had blurted out the words without even knowing she was going to say them. She didn't know where they came from, but she knew she meant what she said. Going to Hawaii with her dad and Eve would solve all her problems, and it would be wonderful to live with her father again. Dana felt a great sweep of relief now that she had made her decision.

"Did you hear me, Dad?" she said, excited now. "My answer is yes!"

"Did I ever! Oh, Dana, that's wonderful. Thank you, darling. Wait a minute. Eve's here . . . Eve! Eve!" Dana heard him calling. "Dana's decided. She's coming with us. . . . Eve says that's absoutely great," he said, coming back to the phone. "She's as happy as I am, and oh, Dana, honey, I'm so happy I can't begin to tell you *how* happy I am."

"Me, too, Dad. Of course I have to finish up here."

"Oh, sure. We'll work out all the details later. There's plenty of time now that you've decided. Hold on. Eve wants to talk to you."

"Dana?"

"Yeah, Eve."

"I want you to know I'm just delighted."

Dana was getting more excited. "I'm delighted, too. Listen, Eve, what do you wear in Honolulu?"

"I don't have a clue. We'll have to find out together. You think grass skirts?"

Dana laughed. "Only every other Thursday," she said.

"Of course. I forgot," said Eve, also laughing.

Suddenly, all Dana's burdens fell away. It was going to be really terrific to be in Hawaii. She was going to love being with her father, and Eve was going to be fun and nice, too.

Her father was back on the phone. "A big hug, Dana!"

"Same to you, Dad. See you in June."

"I'll talk to you before I go back to Honolulu."

"Okay, Dad. Bye. Say good-bye to Eve. Say . . . I send my love to Eve," Dana said.

She hung up and walked away from the phone booth almost in a daze.

I'm not coming back to Canby Hall next year, she said to herself as she crossed the lounge. *I'm going to live with my father in Honolulu*, she added in her head as she went out the door. She had wanted out and now she'd be out. She wouldn't have to cope with Shelley anymore. She would be far away from all the things that had been making her so miserable and unhappy. They would all disappear, and in addition, she'd have all the adventure of being in Hawaii.

Then, painfully, another thought struck her. *I have to tell Mom.* First, though, Dana went to Addison House to tell Nancy, who simply shook her head.

"I'm in shock," she said.

"I feel kind of weak in the knees myself," Dana said.

"Wow." Nancy shook her head again, as if to clear it.

"Yeah, I know." Dana laughed tensely.

"You decided just like that?" Nancy asked.

"Yes. I didn't even know I *had* decided."

"A whole year in Hawaii and not here. It'll be awful without you, but, oh, Dana," Nancy said, "you'll see beautiful colors. Lucky you."

"You know what else, Nancy?" Dana leaned forward in the bean-bag chair. "Everything's okay now. The thing is, there's just no point in coming back to Canby Hall. In Hawaii I won't have the problem of Shelley ever again."

"Dana, if that's all it is, you can room with me next year."

"Yes, but I'd see her on the campus. I'd

always be afraid I'd run into her. I couldn't stand a whole year avoiding her like I do now, and I couldn't stand being with her. I *have* to leave Canby Hall."

That evening, Room 407 was filled with that awful, formal quiet that haunted it during Study Hours. Dana, Shelley, and Faith were in the room, each at work. As soon as the sudden noise of doors banging open, loud voices, and footsteps in the hall announced that Study Hours were over, Shelley gathered a scattered pile of papers and got up.

"I'm going to the lounge," she said to Faith, glancing at Dana from the corner of her eye. "I want to finish this book report, and it'll be easier to work down there."

Dana lifted her eyebrows. Then she frowned. She hadn't been able to concentrate very well on tracing the course of the Nile, her assignment for social studies. She thought she would feel permanently relieved having made her decision to join her father and Eve in Hawaii, but back in Room 407, it was still a tense situation. She had told Faith and Shelley her news, but the conversation about it had been very brief. Shelley's mouth dropped open and her eyes widened, but she didn't say a word.

"I'm sorry to hear that, Dana," Faith had said. "I'll miss you." That was all.

Dana stopped working and turned in her chair. "Do you hate me, Faith?" she asked.

"Of course not."

As her mother advised, Faith was trying to wash her hands of the problem between her roommates. During the day, between classes, and on weekends, she was spending most of her time with Grace and other girls she knew from the *Clarion* and her classes. Every once in a while she wondered about next year. Maybe she would move into another dorm, take a single, maybe she didn't want roommates at all anymore.

"I'm worried about Shelley, but if you want to know the truth, I've about had it up to here, and it makes me very sad." Faith straightened things on her desk.

"Well, I won't be here next year, so you won't have the problem anymore," Dana said wistfully.

"Oh, Dana, come off it. I'll miss you a lot. You know that. Maybe we just all need our summer vacations."

The girls undressed, got into bed, and turned the lights out, but neither of them were ready to go to sleep.

"I will *not* worry about either of you," Faith muttered into the darkness.

Dana lay thinking of the decision she had made, wondering about next year in Honolulu. She wished Faith could come to Hawaii, too. To her astonishment, she found that she wished Shelley could also come. *Crazy!* she thought. But if Shelley came to Honolulu, she would probably forget about her great acting career, about Tom, and not give the performance, which would be a great relief, almost a service, to everybody who knew her. With that thought, Dana fell asleep.

CHAPTER SEVENTEEN

*D*own, *down, down* her grades were going, and Shelley finally just didn't know what to do.

She left her last period class that day, which was algebra. Even in algebra she realized she was not doing very well. She had just gotten a paper back with a *C* plus, and that almost cheered her up, except she remembered that earlier in the year her algebra grades were *A* minus. This was the first time she had had any mark as low as a C.

That afternoon she did not have to go to special study and she made her way from Main Building over to the library, toward the auditorium. They were rehearsing on stage for the first time. *That should be fun,* she thought to herself as she trudged along the campus. But now she was beginning to get really distressed. Nothing was much fun.

Math was her best subject. If she was getting low marks in math . . .

The thing was, she didn't want to fail in school. She reviewed in her mind how she was doing in every subject. She was just passing math. She was just squeaking by in English, too, but not doing badly. Well, she had to be honest with herself. Maybe she wasn't doing badly in English, but she wasn't doing well. She had done fairly well on the book report, but poorly on her last English test.

Shelley found herself in front of the library, where the auditorium was. She didn't want to go in yet. She didn't want to go to the Student Center. She didn't want to go back to the dorm. She didn't want to talk to anybody. She kept on walking, crossing through the orchard, then sat down facing away from the school buildings, toward the road to the gates, the wrought-iron gates that led out of the school. *I'm not doing well in social studies,* she thought, *and I'm still doing terribly, doing miserably, in French.* She stared at the gates even though she was supposed to be at rehearsal. *French,* she thought. *And the French essay is due tomorrow.*

There was nothing last-minute about it. The class had received the assignment early last week. In fact, Mr. Bernard, three days before, had asked her how it was going, looked at her few notes, encouraged her. "That looks interesting. That's a good beginning," he had said. But Shelley hadn't been able to write one sentence since then.

That night during Study Hours, Shelley tried to organize her work. She decided to write the essay first in English and then translate it. She looked at the notes Mr. Bernard had liked, turned to a clean page in her notebook, and wrote a sentence from the notes at the top of the paper. Then she stopped. What should she write next? Should she write the whole essay in English and then translate it, or write one line in English, one line in French? She had written that first sentence with her regular black felt-tip pen. For the French part, she would use another color. She reached over and took a green felt-tip pen from her collection. She didn't touch the pink and purple pens. They were for writing to Paul and writing home. She hadn't been using them very much lately.

She took the green pen and, under the line she had written in English, slowly wrote a line in French. She went down a few spaces, wrote another line in black, then took up the green pen again, held it, and didn't know what to write. She couldn't do the past tense of verbs! Maybe it would make the essay more interesting if she put it in the present tense.

No, she was doing it all wrong. She tore out the page she had been working on, crumpled it up, turned to a new page, took up the black felt-tip again, and stared at the paper. She felt paralyzed. She picked up her French book and leafed through the vocabulary lists and looked at some of the pages of idioms Dana and Faith had coached her on so hard. Maybe she'd find an appropriate phrase for the next sentence. Maybe she could find whole sentences to use. She carefully read several pages and put the book down. She realized she hadn't understood *anything* she'd read.

Panic set in. She felt she was never going to be able to do the essay. She *had* to do it. It had to be ready tomorrow.

She glanced at Faith and Dana. Faith was at her desk, tipped way back in her chair, absorbed in her textbook. Dana, who had been intent on whatever she was writing at her desk, had just heard the sounds of the end of Study Hours and had lifted her head without turning. *She does that all the time now*, Shelley thought, a spurt of hurt and anger interrupting her anguish about the French essay. Shelley got up. *If I go to sleep right now*, she said to herself, *I'll set the alarm and get up at four in the morning and I'll be fresh and ready to do my essay then*.

Dana closed her notebook and started to walk out of the room, casting a quick glance at Shelley, who still stood at her desk, making the decision to go to bed.

"I'm going down to the Ping-Pong room. Anybody want anything?" Her question was almost reflexive, but she asked it coolly.

Shelley shook her head and Faith said, "No, thanks, I'm visiting Alice and Margie down the hall."

"See you," said Dana, and she went down-stairs where she joined Gloria Palmer for a Tab, and for a moment they thought they might even play Ping-Pong.

In the empty room, Shelley crawled into bed, pulled the sheet up under her chin, and willed herself to go to sleep, but couldn't. After five minutes that seemed like an hour, she got out of bed, picked up her notebook and the green felt-tip pen, and took them back into bed with her. Maybe if she just curled up and worked in bed, she'd be able to do better than she had at the desk.

When Dana came back, Shelley was gone and Faith was already asleep. Shelley wasn't her responsibility, but Dana felt annoyed anyway. *All* of them were supposed to be in their room. After she got into bed, Dana lay listening, waiting, but Shelley didn't come in.

When Dana awoke the next morning, the first thing she saw was Shelley, still in yester-day's clothes, standing in the doorway of the room.

"I had a French essay to write and I fin-ished it," Shelley said in a thin, drained voice. She looked worn and drawn, her usually round and rosy face almost haggard, her great eyes clouded with weariness.

Dana lay there, her hair falling over her face, but Faith rolled out of her bed.

"Good for you," she said gently. "Where have you been?"

"The little room," Shelley answered. Baker House reserved one small room at the end of the hall for girls who wanted to use it for studying, but it was not really supposed to be used after lights out.

Shelley put her notebook and book and pens down on her desk and said, "I think I'm going to take a shower now."

"That's a good idea," Faith said.

After Shelley picked up her towel and left for the bathroom, Dana threw back her covers, stretched, and got up. She avoided it for a moment but then met Faith's eyes. "A for guts," she said finally. "I certainly give her *A* for guts."

CHAPTER EIGHTEEN

The classroom was filled with girls who looked as though they knew what they were doing, as though they knew about French. Shelley's pride in having finished her essay dimmed as she realized the essay wasn't good. It was worse than that. There were probably so many mistakes she would get a zero for it.

Mr. Bernard was collecting the essays, he was leafing through them. He saw hers and looked up over at her and smiled. He glanced at it briefly, then he started to read it more carefully. This time when he looked up — Shelley noticed with a sinking feeling — he didn't smile. *It's awful*, she thought.

Shelley was groggy from staying up all night. She opened her textbook to the day's lesson. The words on the page seemed to shimmer, even though she wasn't being asked to read them. She was lost in some sort of daze. In fact, Mr. Bernard was speaking and she knew she wasn't hearing him correctly. When he finished, the whole class groaned.

"No need for applause," said Mr. Bernard, who was sometimes funny. "You knew you were going to have this test."

"Wasn't it supposed to be *next* week?" Shelley, in shock, asked Molly Jonas, who sat across from her.

"That's what I thought," Molly whispered back.

Shelley put her face in her hands.

Mr. Bernard was explaining. "I've split the final into two parts," he said. "Tomorrow will be vocabulary, perhaps some verb endings, the *avoir* idioms, things you've been going over and over in class and in Language Lab. Next week, as scheduled, will be an essay on France, a review perhaps of some readings. In two parts it is easier for you."

When the class was over, Shelley ran out of Main Building to Baker House and her room. She lay on her bed and began to shiver. She was going to fail and she would be thrown out of school. She would never be able to come back to Canby Hall again. They might not even let her be in the spring play. Tomorrow's test would be filled with exactly what she didn't know. She picked up her workbook. No, that wasn't any good. She scrambled through her notebook. There they were, Dana's lists for vocabulary—the foods, the things in a room, the things in a store, all in Dana's neat writing, English and French, side by side. The idioms she was supposed to know, the verbs they had studied in class were in the textbook, easy to find. *If I only could memorize them,* Shelley thought. *If I have a theatrical memory, why can't I memorize these dumb things?*

Shelley felt weak and she was trembling. She went over to her bureau, picked up the picture of her mother and father in the elaborate brass frame with the brass bowknot on top, and gazed at it mournfully. She thought of how proud her parents were of her, how proudly they had seen her off east to Canby Hall. *How proud would they be now?* she wondered. *I'm going to fail a course and they'll never be proud of me again. I won't disgrace them,* she thought. *I can't!* She was exhausted. She was frightened. She put the picture back, reached out, touched it, then turned away from the smaller picture of Paul that was also on the bureau. She couldn't think about Paul.

Shelley tried to concentrate on French. She *tried* to memorize the rules she didn't know. "In the placement of personal pronouns: the personal pronoun comes before the verb. The only exception is the affirmative command." Shelley tried to review personal pronouns, but she almost couldn't remember the difference between *le* and *la*. Her mind seemed blank. And she knew she had never been able to remember all the *avoir* idioms.

There was only one thing she could do.

Shelley thought about it for a while intently, her chin on her fist, her lips trembling only a little. Then she began to prepare. First she took several sheets of paper out of her notebook and folded them lengthwise once, then twice. Then she borrowed the scissors from Faith's desk and carefully cut the paper into strips. The strips were about an inch wide.

When that was done, Shelley went to her drawer and carefully chose a sweater to wear the next day. It was almost her favorite, even though Dana didn't like it very much, not that that mattered. It was a red cotton cardigan with two big pockets on each side and long sleeves that folded back to make deep cuffs. Shelley quietly opened the door, made sure nobody was coming, and closed it again. She stacked three cans of diet sodas against the door so that if somebody did open it, there'd be plenty of warning clatter. Then she tucked a batch of strips into the cuffs of the sweater. The strips were too long. They showed. Picking up the scissors again, she cut the strips in half, and tucked them again into the cuffs of the sweater. The cuffs concealed them easily now. She also put the strips in the pockets. They were hidden there, too. She put on the sweater over the one she was wearing and practiced sneaking the slips out of the pockets, out of the sleeves, and quickly slipping them back in again. Then, huddled over her desk, her face frozen, Shelley set herself to the task of neatly, clearly, in block letters, copying Dana's lists, copying the idioms, preparing for tomorrow's test. *Preparing to cheat.*

The blue books they used at Canby Hall for tests were passed out and the test began. Shelley bit her lip and closed her eyes. She remembered what Tom had said last week when she was worrying about the French final.

"Sure you'll pass," he had said. "You've been talking about French and working on French and worrying about French for so long, I bet you know more French than most French people do."

"*J'ai peur,*" she had said, almost automatically. "I'm afraid."

Shelley opened the test and looked at the questions. She uncapped her pen, held it in the air for a moment, and attacked. To her surprise, many answers jumped onto the page for her. She picked and chose, filling in where she felt almost sure, pretty sure. Then the questions seemed to get harder, and the verb forms and idioms and vocabulary, French into English, started to have the totally unfamiliar quality she had felt when she read her textbook, when she went through her reader, when she looked at her workbook. It was as though she had never before seen the words. She couldn't remember anything!

Shelley folded her arms on the desk in front of the blue book, so the fingers of her left hand were near the cuff of her right sleeve. Slowly, she slid her fingers into the cuff, caught the slips of paper on which she had written idioms, and began to draw them out. She stared at the blue book, concentrating with all her strength on the step she was taking. The slips of paper were out. If she glanced down *now*, she would have the answers she needed and pass her French test.

It might have happened in a second. It felt like an hour frozen in time. One moment Shelley had some slips of paper in her fingers, hidden by the palm of her hand, ready for a sneaking look. Then her conscience said no. *I can't*, she cried silently. The next moment she crumpled the papers up and was thrusting them into the pocket of her red cardigan, unread. Suddenly, Mr. Bernard was standing beside her with his hand held out.

"I'll take those, Michelle," he said softly.

"I didn't look at them, Mr. Bernard," Shelley said as she drew her hand out of her pocket and gave him the crumpled papers.

"You may leave the room now. Please meet me at my office in one hour."

"But I saw you take the papers from your pocket, Shelley," Mr. Bernard said, sitting behind his desk in the French department office.

"No, you didn't. Honestly, Mr. Bernard, I

was putting them *into* my pocket." Shelley started to cry. "I know I shouldn't have . . ."

"That's so, Shelley. You should *not* have cheated . . ."

"I didn't," Shelley protested hopelessly.

Mr. Bernard sat back in his chair, lowered his chin, and peered at her.

"The papers were in your hand, Shelley."

"*Please*, Mr. Bernard. *I didn't look at them.*"

The teacher shook his head slowly.

"I can't do anything about it, Shelley. I'm very sorry. There aren't many absolute rules at Canby Hall, but we all know how Miss Allardyce feels about cheating."

Miss Allardyce! The headmistress!

"Don't, Mr. Bernard," Shelley begged.

"She would like to see you this evening at seven o'clock."

Shelley slowly lifted her tearstained face to Mr. Bernard. He nodded seriously, his disappointment in Shelley showing clearly in his expression.

"This is worse than just failing, isn't it?" she said with a catch in her throat. Without waiting for an answer, she left the room.

CHAPTER NINETEEN

Dana, Nancy, and Doris Moss, one of Nancy's friends, were finishing off a completely satisfactory afternoon eating several pizzas in town before heading back to school. It had been a shopping expedition in honor of Dana's going to Hawaii. Its special purpose had been to find a present for Eve.

"Let's look at it again," said Doris.

Dana obliged by digging into one of the shopping bags and taking out a plastic box in which rested a smiling, plastic doll in a bright orange, plastic grass skirt. Dana opened the box, took the doll out, and carefully stood it on the table. The movement made the orange plastic streamers of the skirt sway and the doll's head wiggle from side to side.

"I didn't realize it danced!" Doris exclaimed with delight.

Nancy tilted her head to one side and

studied the doll as though she might want to paint it. "Stunning," she finally declared with a straight face.

They all laughed.

"If Eve's the person you say she is, she'll love it," Nancy said.

"I hope so," Dana said. "I can't think of a good name, though. Any suggestions?"

"How about Lulululupulupula?" Doris said, and they all laughed again.

Dana put the dancing doll securely back in its plastic box and the girls gave their attention to the business of pizza, heavy on the sausage, talking, as they had done all afternoon, about Dana's glamorous immediate future.

They parted on the walk at the dorms, Nancy and Doris going on to Addison House, Dana turning into Baker. Dana was eager to show the girls — Faith, Jackie, Gloria — the doll and the big, elaborate book of photographs of Hawaii that she had bought. She was going to show the book particularly to Faith — she was sure Faith would like it — then she was going to give it to her as an early going-away present, a souvenir so Faith wouldn't forget her.

As Dana came into the dorm, she saw Faith walking through the lower hall looking extremely somber. Before she could call out, Faith had disappeared in the direction of Alison's apartment. *That is strange*, Dana thought. She glanced into the lounge. Gloria, Casey, Jackie, and a few other girls were huddled together, speaking in hushed voices. When they saw her, they seemed to huddle even more. Something was very wrong. Dana looked around. A couple of other girls were sitting together silently, as serious as Faith had seemed.

"What's going on?" Dana asked quickly. Her voice sounded inappropriately sharp and clear in the room. "What happened?" she whispered. "Did somebody die?"

Jackie separated herself from the group and came over to her.

"I don't know how you'll feel about this, Dana," Jackie said. "Shelley's sort of in trouble."

"Shelley? Trouble how?" Dana asked, instantly on her guard.

"They say that Mr. Bernard caught her cheating on her French test."

Dana's response burst from her. "Impossible! Shelley wouldn't cheat."

"But you know how it is with her and French," Gloria said.

"But Shelley wouldn't," Dana insisted indignantly.

"Mr. Bernard caught her looking at notes," Gloria said.

"*No.*" Dana's voice was even firmer.

"The papers were right in her hand. She was caught in the act," Jackie chimed in.

"I still don't believe it," Dana said stubbornly. "Where's Shelley now?"

"Upstairs. Getting ready."

"For what?"

"She has to see Miss Allardyce at seven o'clock."

"Oh, no!" Dana said, starting toward the stairs. "I've got to see her."

"I thought you hated Shelley," Casey called after her.

"So did I," Dana answered, running upstairs, her shopping bags swinging.

Dana opened the door of 407. Shelley was standing in the middle of the room, ashen but dry-eyed, dressed neatly in her denim skirt and the pale blue sweater Dana had long ago insisted she buy. Dana dropped the shopping bags on the floor and the two girls faced each other, motionless and silent. Then Dana spoke.

"I heard and I don't believe it," she said.

"I didn't cheat," Shelley said quietly. "I was going to, but I didn't."

Dana came into the room now, full of energy, full of indignation, full of support.

"You *couldn't* cheat."

Shelley shook her head. "I almost did," she said.

"But you didn't. That's what matters. What happens now?"

It was as though Dana had forgotten there ever had been trouble between them, forgotten everything about Hawaii.

"I have to see Miss Allardyce at seven,"

Shelley said. Dana saw Shelley's lips held tight, the clear eyes with no hint of tears, the control. Even Shelley's blond curls seemed restrained as she bent her head to look at her watch. "I have to go over right away."

Dana was swept with compassion. "I'll go with you."

"No, I want to do this alone."

Just then Faith burst into the room.

"She has to go to Allardyce right away, but she doesn't want us to go with her," Dana said to Faith immediately.

Faith hadn't known what to expect when the girls downstairs told her that Dana had come back to the dorm and rushed to Shelley when she heard the news. Now she knew it was all right.

"It's her decision to make," Faith said calmly. "I've been talking to Alison, Shelley. She says Miss Allardyce is always fair. Just tell her what really happened."

Shelley took a deep breath. "I wanted to pass the test so I wrote out those notes, but I didn't look at them," she said.

As Shelley made her way to the door, Dana put her hand out to stop her.

"Shelley, will you forgive me for having been —"

"Dana, will you forgive me?"

"I didn't mean those things I said —"

"You can have your reconciliation later!" Faith interrupted impatiently. "Shelley, go on! Don't be late. And don't be scared."

"We'll see you afterward," Dana said.

"Last chance for company," Faith said with an encouraging smile. "Are you sure you don't want us with you for moral support?"

"Positive."

"Good luck, Shel," Faith said, hugging her.

"Me, too," Dana said. She and Shelley hugged and smiled tremulously at each other.

After Shelley left, Faith slumped into a chair and looked up at Dana. "She's in terrible trouble," Faith said. "I mean she may be tossed out of school."

"Not if she didn't actually do it."

"My dad used to talk about 'circumstantial evidence.' Shelley's case is full of it. Mr. Bernard is positive he saw Shelley taking those stupid notes out of the pocket of her sweater."

"Do you really think it's possible that Shelley will be expelled?" Dana asked, shocked.

"Don't tell me you've forgotten the lioness tradition," Faith answered sardonically.

Dana shook her head. "I wish there were something we could do."

"Well, there isn't. We just have to wait and hope." Faith sighed and slowly hoisted herself up. "How about we hit the salad bar in the dining hall, to kill time?"

Listlessly, unhappily, they left the dorm. There were so many things to say that they didn't say anything. In silence, they scuffled along the walk in front of the dorms, their hearts and thoughts so much with Shelley they didn't even see Molly Jonas until she practically bumped into them.

"Hi. I was just coming to your room to see Shelley. Is she there?" Molly asked.

"No, she's not," Faith said.

"Sorry I missed her." Molly joined them walking. "Boy, that was a gas in French today," she said, laughing. "I've seen terrible attempts at cheating in my time but nothing compared to Shelley's. I was coming over to show her how." She laughed again.

"It's not funny, Molly," Dana said.

"Sure it is," Molly answered. "Shelley's so inept. She took those notes out of the cuff of her sweater, crumpled them in her hand, and stuffed them into her pocket. She didn't even *look* at them."

Dana and Faith stopped dead in their tracks.

"How do you know that?" Dana demanded.

"I saw it. I was looking right at her." Molly looked at Dana's face, then at Faith's. "Hey, listen, nothing happened to her about that, did it? I heard Bernard say he wanted to talk to her later. I figured she explained it to him."

"Wrong!" said Dana. "She's with Allardyce this minute."

"You mean *Allardyce*? About *today*?" Molly gasped.

"She might be expelled," Dana said desperately.

"Will you tell Allardyce what you just told us?" Faith demanded of Molly.

"Well . . ." Molly hesitated. "I never had a face-to-face with Allardyce. I had hoped to finish my Canby Hall career without that pleasure, but . . ."

"Molly," Dana said. "You're wasting time."

"The whole thing's a joke. Of course I'll tell what I saw. I was coming over to laugh about it with Shelley, wasn't I?"

The three girls changed course instantly, Dana and Faith hurrying Molly between them in the direction of the headmistress's house.

Miss Allardyce was as relieved as the girls were after they were admitted to the little office in her residence and Molly told her story. Miss Allardyce started talking about seriousness and honesty and lionesses, but Shelley looked so strained, wan, exhausted, that the headmistress actually cut her lecture short and sent the girls back to their dorms.

They left the house quickly, as though it were haunted, as though they had to escape from it, to separate themselves from the reason Shelley had been there. Stumbling, falling all over each other, they made their way across the velvety lawns of the headmistress's house and into the birch grove, which was their shortcut back to the dorms.

"If you don't mind," Shelley said suddenly, "I'm going to sit down for a moment. My legs aren't working," and she plopped down under a tree.

"No wonder," Faith said.

Shelley began to shake.

"Isn't this dumb?" she said, her voice fluttering as she hugged herself tightly to try to stop shivering. Faith and Dana both put their arms around her to warm her up, to make the trembling stop.

"It's over now, Shel," Faith said.

Shelley shook her head. "Only the cheating part," she answered, her voice still uncertain, her body still shaking.

"Hey, Shelley?" Molly said. She was confused at the intense emotion the other girls seemed to be feeling. "You okay?"

Shelley turned her shivering into a series of nods and smiled weakly at Molly.

"Molly, you're the special hero," Dana said. "We're all grateful to you. You were really terrific, you know, the way you handled old Allardyce in her den."

"Well, what's the point of being a lioness if you can't be brave once in a while?" Molly asked.

"I appreciate it a lot, Molly." Shelley was calmer now, hardly shaking.

"We're going to do something for you, Molly," Dana said.

"What?" asked Molly, smiling.

Dana hesitated. "I don't know yet," she said. "Give you a present."

Faith looked at her watch. "There's a chance we're going to get into some new trouble if we don't get back to our dorms," she said. "Are you ready to get up, Shelley?"

"Sure." Shelley still felt a tremendous weakness of vast relief, but she had stopped shaking and her legs were all right. The girls got up from the grass under the birches, brushed themselves off, and continued on their way. As they walked in the silent evening, Dana was thinking about what had happened and how she felt. She realized that she had decided to live with her father partly because the Shelley business had made her so unhappy. Now the reason wasn't true anymore.

She loved her father, even liked Eve, but that was not why she had been going to Hawaii.

"Wait," Dana commanded as they reached Baker House. "I have to get something. Stay right there. Don't move."

She dashed into the dorm and came out again quickly, carrying the present she had bought that afternoon.

"This is for you," she said, placing the Hawaiian dancing doll in Molly's hands, "with the eternal appreciation of all the girls in Room 407, Baker House, Canby Hall."

Faith and Shelley were both surprised and their eyes met. Neither of them had seen the doll before, but they knew it had to do with Dana's decision to go to live in Hawaii. Dana had it and now she was giving it away.

Dana, Faith, and Shelley walked Molly back to her dorm.

In their own dorm, they tried to go quietly

up the stairs to their room. It was the middle
of Study Hours and they had been out later
than they were supposed to be. But it didn't
do any good to tiptoe. All the girls on their
floor seemed to be gravitating anxiously into
the hall, but when they saw the three girls
they knew without being told that the awful
evening had ended all right. Alison came out
of her apartment and she was relieved, too,
by what she saw with her quick glance. She
then sent all the girls to their rooms.

"It's still Study Hours," she announced.

In 407, Dana, Shelley, and Faith were together again. There was a hush in the air as
they realized what had happened in the past
few hours.

"I owe you lots of thanks," Shelley said to
both her roommates.

"But I owe you lots of apologies, Shelley,"
Dana said slowly.

"Oh, we both weren't so wonderful," Shelley said.

The girls looked seriously, somberly at
each other, knowing that in a time of crisis
they had shown how they had felt about each
other.

"But I said such awful things!" Dana
groaned at the thought.

"Well, so did I," Shelley said. "I guess we
were so upset about other things, we lashed
out at each other."

Faith took a deep breath. "There are still those other things," she said.

Shelley sat at her desk and stared for a moment at the papers there, her French book, the notebook, the French workbook, all still in a jumble as she left them, still bearing in their messiness the reflection of how she had felt. She thought of the makeup French test Miss Allardyce said she would be able to take.

"In the funniest way, I don't think it's going to be so bad anymore. I'm not going to flunk French," she said. "I'm sure of that. I'll work harder. I won't goof off. I know I can do it!" She paused and then went to the pictures on her bureau. "I still love Paul, you know. The only thing is, I love Tom, too. And you know what else?" It was their old Shelley speaking. "I used to think Mr. Bernard was sort of cute, and I may start thinking that again."

Shelley became serious again and looked up at Dana. "Don't forget, though, I also love acting, I love being in the spring play. Later on, I really may be an actress, a great actress, if I can be. But . . ." Dana and Faith were quiet as they listened to Shelley, as they looked at her round face just getting some of its color back, her tangle of blond hair, her bright eyes now shadowed by the day and these new thoughts. "The main thing is, I don't have to decide now, do I?"

"Nope," said Faith.

"I guess not," said Dana. "I guess absolutely

not." She was settling back on her bed, not much inclined, as none of them were, to do any schoolwork. She kicked off one shoe, pulled her sweater over her head, started toward her T-shirt nightgown, and then suddenly jumped up.

"I almost forgot. I have to call my dad," she said. "I have to tell him I've changed my mind. Next year, I'm not going to be in Hawaii. I'm going to be in Canby Hall — where I belong."